ALSO BY PAUL WEST

FICTION

Love's Mansion
The Woman of Whitechapel and Jack the Ripper
Lord Byron's Doctor
The Place in Flowers Where Pollen Rests
The Universe, and Other Fictions
Rat Man of Paris
The Very Rich Hours of Count von Stauffenberg
Gala
Caliban's Filibuster
Colonel Mint
Bela Lugosi's White Christmas
I'm Expecting to Live Quite Soon
Alley Jaggers
Tenement of Clay

NONFICTION

James Ensor
Portable People
Sheer Fiction I & II
Out of my Depths: A Swimmer in the Universe
Words for a Deaf Daughter
I, Said the Sparrow
The Wine of Absurdity
Byron and the Spoiler's Art

POETRY

The Snow Leopard
The Spellbound Horses

RAT MAN OF PARIS

PAUL WEST

RAT MAN OF PARIS

THE OVERLOOK PRESS
WOODSTOCK • NEW YORK

First published in 1993 by
The Overlook Press
Lewis Hollow Road
Woodstock, New York 12498

Library of Congress Cataloging-in-Publication Data

West, Paul, 1930-
Rat Man of Paris.
I. Title
PR6073.E766R38 1986 813'.54

ISBN: 0-87951-502-3

Without an adversary one cannot be victorious, and for the contest one must arm oneself with unflagging zeal and steadfastness and patience.

JOHANN JOSEPH FUX, *The Study of Counterpoint,* 1725

I
Poussif

One

For what seem to him not very good reasons, he lives on the Street of the Cat Who Fishes, reputed to be the shortest, narrowest street in the world. No doors, only one window, and this is his, if anyone can be said to own a window, which feat of ownership must surely include all the light passing through it. He enters from the other side of the building. The window he has blocked with newspaper, which he never renews until it falls apart. Within, he sleeps on a wide shelf made into a bunk, but the room is higher than wide. The street itself is where locals dump their garbage. Once a month someone comes and hauls it away so that the street can fill up again. One o'clock next week, he tells himself. That's when they come. It is no more reliable or dependable than that.

The very least that can be said of him is that he has moved with the times, grown with them, perfecting his art. In this he resembles one of those prisoners of war who, made to sleep for years in big wooden drawers just long enough to hold a man, found themselves unable to sleep in anything else. His lifestyle is cramped, you might say, but it has flowered in extraordinary fashion.

In the old, postwar days, before his rage mellowed, he worked the streets of the city with a squad of kids, flashed his live rat at the diners and Pernod sippers on the boulevards while the kids picked pockets. In several ways his art was one of distraction. The kids supplied him with the rats, maybe one a month, and of each rat in turn he became quite fond until he set it free, usually in Pigalle, with a brisk tap of his foot. The rats never came back, and of course the odds against his getting the same rat to work with again were vast. Yet some of them seemed oddly familiar to him, and he could never be sure, so he treated them all as old allies. Never has he been bitten.

In those early days he believed it possible to haunt the streets twenty-four hours a day, filching food and sleeping in famous graveyards. Always on call while the rest of the world, the kids included, worked eight-hour shifts, he wanted to be there. Usable. Available. A local celebrity, though according to him if you were a celebrity in Paris you were of world importance.

Poulsifer, alias Rat Man, seemed to be everywhere, a post-war apparition both harsh and playful, reminding the world of what it had recently gone through, but also making fun of the trauma too. A Rat Man could amuse.

The kids soon learned how to do without him, though, thrusting big cardboard signs of atrocious pathos at those whose pockets they picked. Those undisposed to give ended up giving anyway. It was the kids who told his name, as it were depriving him of his title and his fame, but Poulsifer endured, suddenly willing to do odd jobs to keep body and soul on nodding terms, and flashing his rats for their own sake, almost like some middle-aged mother with her newest-born: pink nose and unformed mouth.

Flashing a baby, he knew back then, would have been almost as good as flashing a rat, but it would have been more difficult to arrange. And a baby, being human, would have sharpened his sadness.

Something in plastic, then, or a salmon carved in wood. A doll. A bowling pin. A flute.

The gesture was what mattered: the sudden, almost voluptuous exposing of the head. He was a man who had World War Three cradled in his arms. The quick glimpse was more than enough for most of those he accosted. He unnerved them and went his way, averaging some fifty daily. Who could have asked for more? If he kept it up for twenty-four hours, that was roughly two per hour, and of course he had to walk a lot, then brood on his art, and eat, and plan, and eavesdrop, not to mention sleeping standing up like a horse, in a graveyard or not.

That was Poulsifer then, pretty much Poulsifer now, except that he has become more self-conscious, less impetuous. He still hunts the perfect demeanor for what he does with his rats. He envisions the correct degree of limp, the just-so pouncing movement as he reveals the off-color pink of the nose. He dreams of the perfect accost, aiming at his victim from as much as a minute's walk away, and heading forward in a stumble-totter that culminates with him erect and proud. He flips his coat open, watches them recoil or laugh, then backs off, shaking his head. He says nothing at all. Insults, coins, rolled-up newspapers, come after him, but by then he is on his way to someone else.

He likes to vary his targets.

As he sees it, he is molesting no one at all.

There is no humor in it. The whole thing is a demonstration, a ritual. Far from trying to shock the bourgeoisie, he thinks of himself as tweaking the race. Helping it evolve.

Surely it is dead, they say of the rat, but he is good at maneuvering the head, so they never quite know if he has or has not a live beast against his shirt. Not that big, oh no, but unexpected and therefore looming large.

Those who know him well, by sight anyway, know what to expect. They think he varies his act. Now a live rat, now one dead. Now one stuffed with sawdust and swathed in sealskin. Now one he can make move by squeezing a rubber ball.

Still, adept as he is, he is ready for a new interest in life. Something is always rumbling beneath him, maybe the future. Were this an alp he lived on, such rumbling might be an avalanche, but the noise is that of Paris doing its usual horizontal tumble on all sides of him.

It does not disturb where the rat lives. In distant days he housed his rat in a shoe box or an orange crate, but for some years now he has provided a doll's house in which a tiny derelict bed, a dust-laden miniature table, chairs Thumbelina-sized, give the rat a landscape to dominate. Surely the rat feels huge. In each chair he has fixed a fluff of cotton to simulate a person lounging or sitting erect, and it is among these ghosts that the off-duty rat moves. Rat Man peers in and, for a moment, almost believes that the doll's house is full of small people, especially if he blurs his eyes. The rat dislodges nothing, and Rat Man sometimes wonders if that is because the toy furniture, the puff-cotton people, exist only in his mind's eye. This is when he lifts the hinged roof and touches the things within. The rat, even if on the bottom floor, scampers upstairs to be fed, only to find Rat Man engaged in something too private to admit a rat. The whole doll's house smells of rotting corn.

The rat has an easy life, comparatively speaking.

But several rats have left him, and that gives him an opportunity to use a fake one, marveling at how still it lies in the doll's house, in a perpetual taxidermist's slumber he envies. Perhaps once a month, whether the house's inmate is a live one or a dud, he walks the long way round into the Street of the Cat Who Fishes and dumps out the corn and the droppings on top of the other garbage, then reaffixes the lid of the roof and starts all over again. Seen in this act, though by few, he appears to be some irate giant smashing up a village, street by street, house by house, but the toy furniture is glued in place and the fuzzy people too. He likes things to be where they belong. Oddly enough, the doll's house is one of the few things which survived the demolition of the village in which he grew up, after which for quite a while it was no longer a place in which to do anything at all. He sometimes envisions the doll's house on fire, ablaze within while the walls remain intact. The dolls are screaming.

Then he eases his mind by tabulating various forms of rats, wondering why there has been no chronological development from real to fake, or vice versa, from less and less realistic model rats to wholly abstract ones. But no, he muddles along, ringing the changes according to whim. He uses numbers nonetheless, as if to suggest progress:

1. Real rats, white or gray
2. Rubber rats
3. Papier-mâché
4. Wooden or clay
5. Dead, real rats
6. Guinea pigs or bloated mice
7. The fox

This last is what his mind turns to more and more, though he quivers when he looks at it for very long. His mother's, it must once have been a real live fox. It even has claws, a snout, and its fur is the softest thing he has ever felt except for his mother's hair. There are even small loops of velvety cord with which to keep the fox in place around one's neck, and these he uses to fasten the fox to one of the top buttonholes in his shirt. Two feet long, it makes an imposing rat.

How odd, he thinks. If I were Fox Man, even rats would look like foxes. It all goes with the name. Foxes are close enough, in rough general appearance, to rats anyway, whereas with miniature horses the illusion would break down.

So he accepts it, this being a master illusionist, whom the people at the café tables resent only a bit more than they enjoy. Had he not become Rat Man, someone else would have. Dimly aware of some cause, he thinks the source of his role is in trying to express the faint, doomed quality of the fuzzy creatures who loll in the chairs in the doll's house. Like ourselves, he decides, they are hardly here at all. One puff removes them. It is so easy.

Then he realizes something else. Those quick glimpses of the thing inside his coat match, more or less, the thing he sees ahead of him. The black horizon of becoming sixty, seventy, if he is lucky. Some slow, hardly visible shove guides him onward to its edge. As if he were on a glacier, feet frozen to its surface and unable to walk back. His body moves forward, but his mind ducks back. He retreats from both the past and the future, and his meager life is an attempt not to cooperate with even the present.

He adds up his world and it does not come to much. Maybe a few extra colors or sounds will drift into it. A new taste. New aches and pains to be sure, but nothing big. He gropes for a new word. Big is not right. Classic, then. Or monumental. Perched on the floor by the doll's house, he looks up and sees what crosses the room above him: a thin frayed cord to which he means to fasten with clothespins what he tears from newspapers and magazines. Except that he never gets around to doing it: repeatedly, his hand will lift to make the first tear, but the piece always looks better off marooned in the surrounding newsprint. Best forget it rather than make it semi-permanent on the line, upon which, instead of newsprint, it is fluff that gathers, like some mellow frost of fatigue.

The whole thing would be far too easy, he decides. Stick things on a line and they belong together, or seem to. It is much harder to disconnect things from one another. Easier to charm sperm from out of the Sphinx than separate the Sphinx from Egypt. He warms to the idea. He lets things begin that, once let loose, will have their way with him all day. Cigar butts in the gutters rise up and fly like bees. An entire pig, sliced up and reassembled in a butcher's window, with each section outlined in red, begins to fall apart again because the ground is rumbling: first the forefeet down the gentle gradient of white tile, then the head, sagging at the snout.

Two

To ready himself for an afternoon's or an evening's work, he has to soothe himself. He does not like to go out feeling ragged or frayed. Nowadays, after having let the habit slide for years, he once again uses his magnifying glass, breathes hard on the glass before polishing, then takes up a handful of travel brochures. Over these he pores, examining beaches and terraces for loudspeakers and portable radios. Each time he finds one, he lets out a satisfied whistle of disgust. No place is safe, no haven is quiet. He decides, as always, to stay where he is. He feels vindicated. He would like to go elsewhere, but every brochure tells a story, and every map kills him with things he hates to find next to what he has to put up with anyway. Railroads. Superhighways. Gas stations. Traffic lights. Small hamlets of cops. He would love the beaches, the terraces, but there is always something wrong with them.

He has in mind some strand of pink or white, or even post-volcanic black. There need not even be sand. A rubble beach will serve. It can only be found, he is beginning to believe, at a higher altitude, eternally smothered in cloud. No way up, no way down. Not really there at all.

So he lives as he does where he is, although with a sense of having simplified his life beyond recall.

What astounds him about people is the way they go about their daily chores quite unsurprised at being alive. Or at least by remaining for so long in a state very different from dead. He expects them to stand or sit aghast on the boulevards, stunned by the sheer joy of it, by the wash of gladness numbing them. Unable to speak or gesture but thrilled to bits because they can say to themselves: This is it. This is mine, so far. We are all of us alive without having done anything to bring our own lives into being.

He has felt this ever since the Liberation of Paris, against whose backdrop he still resees the gruesome civilities of the first Nazis to arrive.

For hours, he sits savoring the magic of being Poulsifer, who might be a thousand other beings than Rat Man. In his day he has made ends meet by blowing soap bubbles in a forward-looking nightclub and cunningly filling them, or parts of them, with cigarette smoke. That is one of his livings. No one pays him much for anything, although tourists have offered unusual sums to him to take his rat away. But he makes no deals. He reserves the right to return. He is an informal institution, a lump of local color. His photograph sits unlooked at, after once being shown, in Oslo, Bethlehem, and Bonn. People are glad to get home from where he lurks.

I am Rat Man of Paris, he tells himself, with just a touch of miserable awe. That is all they know about me. Even when I die, for several years I will not be dead. They will think I am taking a month off. The tourists will never know, only the locals.

He is also Poulsifer, of course, son of Alsatian parents who, resenting the German flavor of their native region, moved all the way to Limoges, in west-central France. After the war, perhaps obeying some echo in his head, he worked for a year with a team that raised crashed aircraft from the seabed or the bottoms of lakes. Messerschmitts among them. Scrap or souvenir. His own job, after the raising, was to hose out the cockpits and retrieve the bones, which he would hand out like someone unpacking the latest in Fischer-Technik erector sets. Basic kit without motor, he liked to say. Fifty or more pieces.

Then he tired of dredged-up planes.

The bones began not to sicken him.

So he cast about for something else, convinced that, whatever else it did, the soul should be eloquent. He studied the habits of the Masai. Learned to roller-skate. Became a janitor at a travel agency. Sold balloons in the streets. He was always looking for the thing that would send a thrill through him; the thing which, though only a part of life, reminded him of life's whole. And found it in no thing but in Sharli Bandol, who taught high school and still does. To her, he is Poussif because, if she says his surname fast, that is how it sounds. Thus her own mother's name, Madeleine, had dwindled into Madly.

She meets him for the first time over and over again. Going home early, she has paused for a cup of coffee, but she is peckish, so she orders a ham sandwich. While she stares into the middle distance, munching, or halting altogether with the unchewn morsel behind her teeth, here comes this aloof-looking man with the used-looking face. Now he pauses in front of her and pops his rat. She is so tired that she does not flinch, but, almost in a reflex, pulls a bit of bread loose and offers it to the pink nose of the rat, which does not move.

Dead? she asks.

Worse, he says. Inanimate. It's got no soul.

Perplexed, she drops the bread bit to the street, wondering why the man bothers. He gets his effect, then cancels it. It must be how he picks up girls, although this one looks less like a picker-up of girls than a starer-down of trucks. The big, rather round face includes several expressions, all neuter or numb. He begins to smile, but seems unable to go on. He says an opening word, but loses heart in what comes next. He lifts a hand as if to motion, then lets it sink to his side. All the same, he looks worth teasing out. Impromptu, she thinks. He wishes not to have to think things out beforehand. Then why the rat or whatever it is? She asks. He yawns as if this has been asked of him a thousand times, sits down by her, and says there is no simple answer.

Again ordering that ham sandwich when all she meant to pause for was a cup of coffee, she stares into the much-used middle distance, munching or halting with the unchewn morsel behind her teeth, vaguely thinking about the lovers in the English poem about a Grecian urn, and here comes this punished-looking face, like something painted on a balloon but which has come off the balloon and floats about free on its own, a daub aloft. When she sees the rat and asks if it is dead, not so much in a spirit of inquiry as to make vacant conversation, she sees her hand floating a bit of bread toward the rat before the answer comes.

Oh, a dud, she says dreamily.

Like its owner.

You *own* the rat, monsieur?

We belong to each other, madame. We have each other, the dead man and the dud rat.

I suppose I have to pay you to take it away.

I'll take it away for free. As I see it, folks pay me to bring it to them, but they don't know that. I have to take the liberty. If you told them beforehand that Etienne Poulsifer, boulevard notable, was coming toward them with his rat, they'd all scatter. So I presume they have already paid. Then we are free to go ahead. The coins they hand over are really a very late *deposit.* If you think on folks' behalf, they usually turn up trumps. Now, would you rather pay to see the rat or see it go away? Which strikes you as more positive? I never met one yet who thought it positive to go away. Life is built like that. It's all in the approaching. I have often wondered, marching the streets, if I would ever see some face as grand as yours at one of the tables. A cheerful, sensitive face like yours, if you'll pardon the intrusion. You never consult your rat about things like that. You make up your own mind and sail ahead. Followed by a nice *how do you do?* Courtesy went out with one of the big wars, I forget which. Your war is a hotbed of rudeness, *I* say. I am not a picker-up of girls. No, I am a hunter of madonnas. One a year at most. So do you wonder I accost? I most often do not even talk. When I do, though, it's as if people are talking to themselves. They don't believe this apparition is talking to them. So I get no credit for piping up. See how it goes? You approach. They send you away, glad to be rid of you. You open your trap and they think it's all happening in their heads. It takes some breaking through to them. I am real only when going away or remaining silent. Look.

He lights a book match, then puffs it out, sets the charred wisp on a hand-held coin to writhe and cool. Since there is no breeze, the burned match does not blow away. Rat Man of Paris has just burned a match for *her,* and cooled it on a coin. Surely the day has gone awry. It is as if he cooked a morsel of ham right there and proffered it in homage.

See, madame, the match came toward you in its flame. He is still holding it. He snaps the stem and rubs faint charcoal into the coin's face, both sides, making the coin remember. Away goes the unburned bit, somewhere into the late afternoon, and then he pockets the coin. Is he real or not? Who's asking? Sharli feels mesmerized. The man sits down, sips his coffee, looms up all of a sudden in her ordered world. His rat is a fox. She handles it, noting how musty it smells. It smells of attics, mothballs, and old apples. It was his mother's. One day he will tell her about the real rat. Rats plural. He promises. All at once the muscles in one side of his face relax and droop. His speech blurs, then improves. It happens a few times until he explains that he does indeed have little *moments,* no doubt from the strain of always talking to strangers who wish to remain strangers, and of patrolling the boulevards with a fox-fur rat. Telling him to get help, she finds herself mentioning the name of a doctor. No, he says gently, with an almost haughty emphasis, I don't do doctors, I never did, any more than I do tax collectors, clergymen, police, caretakers, janitors, groundsmen, and mailmen.

Do, she says, phrasing her question as a statement: as in have to do with, traffic with, give the time of day to. Myself, I don't do head teachers, gynecologists' receptionists—in fact, I don't do receptionists at all. They're the lowest of the lot.

Museum guards are bad, he says, as if just having discovered them. And you can't say much for the doormen at the big hotels.

They are particularly awful, Sharli agrees: the doormen. But tour guides are the pits.

Tours? I *never* do *tours,* Rat Man tells her. The only tour I'd ever consider is one leading me home to myself. I'd like a tour to me.

Rats, she notes with sleepwalking logic, don't help. They must, well, distract you from yourself. Don't they?

He does not answer, but fondles the fox, almost as if expecting it to bite him. Between finger and thumb he traps the snout shut and does not let it go.

I don't do taxidermists, either, she says.

Yes, he says, people in post offices are awful snippy too. You almost have to go as far as India or China to find anybody with manners befitting a skunk. I don't mean etiquette either, I mean just normal civility, one human to another. As if we all came out of the same womb. There are no ladders in wombs, are there now?

This she ignores, watching the sky turn bruise colors, the lights come on both near and far as if Paris were a galleon setting out for China or India. Something about Rat Man draws her to him, an odd mix of authority and pain. Why should anyone as attuned as he tramp the streets except to prove how useless attunement is? If you are that much out of things, why go on proving it? Unless you want back in more than you want anything. In a sense, she begins to decide, he belongs more to Paris than any Parisian proper. He is strangely *of* the city whereas they are merely *with* it. His heart's in the right place, anyway, buried ten kilometers deep in plutonium-proof concrete embedded in lead and broken glass.

Already they are up and strolling along together, swapping personages or officials they do not *do,* thus dismissing half of the race before they arrive at her place, only two minutes' walk from where she will cook him a sausage and an egg, stir for him a cup of hot chocolate, defrost for him a frozen éclair. All this she does while he marvels, almost *(his* image) like a mongrel being canonized a saint. It has not come his way before, and he welcomes it even if, within the hour, she is going to rope him to the bedstead with stern orders to keep clean for the next three days. (Can Cleopatra be a Gorgon?) Or tie him to a chair, a tree, while spraying him with disinfectant? No, not spray; in those days they swabbed. Some awful memory of childhood is stirring him.

In in one, she laughs. Turn the key and shove.

Out in two, he echoes. Out the window and down into the street. I'm a jumper too, when I set my mind to it.

Potluck, she warns him. I wasn't expecting guests.

I'm only one, Rat Man announces with mellow finality. I don't take up much room. And the rat, he doesn't eat at all. A live one can eat dud food, but a dud can't eat any food at all. Isn't life queer?

Who *is* this man, she wonders, busily talking himself free of ugliness? Plainness, anyway. He's not much to look at. He reminds me of how they stick their heads inside the door in a hospital. A short look is enough. Longer and you might look even worse. That's him: you listen long, you look as quickly as you can. You'd think he'd never talked before.

Almost on cue, Rat Man, already on his fourth glass of red wine, is explaining the economy of France, or of the world. The rich, he says, have to find something to do with all their surplus money, so folks invent things that nobody in their right mind should ever want, and then they make these things compulsory. They live in a halo of frills. If you're poor, though, life presses around you tight. What you don't have hugs you close. Not friendly, either. Like a boa constrictor. Me, I yearn for Guadeloupe. It would just about meet my needs. Here I am in Paris, though. What would Paris be without me? Or you? When I grow up. No, I don't mean that. In a year or two, I'm going to pick a place. Sea close to the promenade that runs along the park where the hotel is. Nobody but deaf-mutes and music lovers. I'll live on ice cream and gently fried shrimp. Bosca wine from Italy. And no newspapers allowed. Fluff would come falling from the sky. You know where Guadeloupe is. Down past Puerto Rico—

She knows. She has taught geography among a dozen subjects, but he seems loath to know, storming on with his vision of a dismal plenty, with his long arms gesturing as if somehow to pull the far-off island into the room through sheer force of personality. Off him comes a smell of burned paper and egg yolks. The arm around her seems heavy with muscle, yet is thin. His voice rumbles always into faintness as if running out of juice, often in the middle of a word. The skin of his hand feels dry but smooth. With more and more wine he goes paler, exuberant but with small rather than expansive smiles. He looks like Baudelaire, but his hair is thicker, and baldness is nowhere in sight. *Baudelaire de lune,* she jokes to herself, but this is one of your nonstop talking daylight men. *Homo* something or other. Who unearthed him? *I* did. It makes you feel like an archaeologist, an anthropologist. I am all sorts of ologists today. How on earth, having retrieved him from the terminal moraine of history, do you get him back where he belongs?

Or not. Something in him appeals to her: it offers itself up and, in the other sense, it meets with her approval. Affectopath, she sometimes calls herself; she hungers for affection, hungers to give it, and he has sensed this, as well as the tang and glint of her. Why, he might even consider installing a woman in his affections in place of a rat, or a fox fur. Two people hungering for affection may end up hungering for each other, quite abstractly to begin with, just as two people hungering to give it would want it all the more. They like to touch, these two. They do not flinch at contact, they always close the gap, if gap there is. Something maternal in her wakes and spreads itself out in his presence, much as something childlike surfaces in him and wants to be looked after.

It is more or less mutual, then. They regale and use each other in the same motion.

Mmm, she murmurs. I could take a lot of this.

Well, he answers, it's for the taking. Give and take, Sharli. As if he has known her for years.

Give a lot, want a lot, she continues. Get a lot, give even more. It flows around.

And then, he says valiantly, it bounces back like the sea. I'd like to have a girlfriend, I really would.

Right, then tell her about you, no holds barred. She wants to know what she is getting into.

If I weren't me, he says, what I do in the streets would be a pretty good way of breaking the ice with total strangers. Absolute strangers, I mean. There is nothing more absolute than a stranger you still haven't spoken to. But, because I really am me, and ever more will be so, I begin by making the contact as if it's all going to lead to something. My life has been a whole series of wasted introductions. I accost people so as to go away. Then they feel even stranger. I go up to them so they'll send me away. Isn't that funny? I'm sociable only in a sort of scientific sense. Nobody has ever discovered my tribe. I'll belong to it when they find it, if ever. Until then, well, I mooch through, cheering myself up with the thought that, one day soon, I'll have to revisit all the places I've been miserable in, just to see if I can be happy in them after all. I'm not wild or mad or backward, I think. I just, as they say, find myself temporarily at a loss. So I do what comes naturally. It wouldn't be natural for anybody else. It's me, though. I used to be Rat Man of Paris. I still am. But I'm different. I've become fed up with my art, my act, and yet I still need it. Etienne Poulsifer, the human being, at your service. Coffee? More? I don't mind. It makes my wrists shake, but the rest of me shakes so much it's nice to have the wrists tuned in.

Something he said about breaking ice with total strangers haunts her. It reminds her of breaking bread with total strangers: a ritual of planetarians which says, yes, we can all be reduced to this, munching on processed wheat. Just a little, he is humanity to her, much as the children she teaches are to her in a more conjectural way. He has no pretenses, no side. He talks intimately as if from a great distance.

I love to talk, he says, being one who never had the chance. I listen too.

Ah, that's it, she says. Talkers are ten a penny. Listeners—well, you can count them on one hand. Get comfy now.

Am, he sighs.

About time, from what you say.

He smells shampoo, the sweetest perfume in years.

She tells him its name. He forgets, but attempts a squeeze. It's like, he says hesitantly, translating all you do into affection. A new language.

She murmurs agreement, and they muse gently on, like two passengers side by side, with hours to spare, looking frontward, having the conversation of their lives, their needs without warning paired.

Three

Whenever they can, and weather allows, they go in her little car to park under the planes landing or leaving at the nearby airport, holding hands as jets or piston engines waft downward across the road, perhaps a hundred meters high. The two of them like to be flown over while they huddle together, murmuring quiet wows and wondering what type plane will come over next. It is like living on a new planet. They feel on the brink of things, not dangerously so, but where the future takes a long hard breath. They have settled down together at almost appalling speed, each drawn to the sheer novelty of the other, each over-endowed with affection. Love-guzzlers they call each other, laughing mildly, delighted with the workings of blind providence. They have been dead more years than they can count. They had been saving themselves up for nobody, and here they are, on each other's doorstep, plighting and replighting their troth to the tune of engines, and flown over, as it were, by thousands of unseeing witnesses, authenticated by a public held in by belts. Watching the planes, they talk about everything and anything, celebrating togetherness in a blaze of free-form prattle.

He tells her, quite often, about how Australians rear baby turtles in plastic pools, and seed oysters with metal disks so as to make pearls. Then, quite often, she tells her children most of this in abbreviated form. She lets him say anything because, most of the time, he talks to himself. So she hears how the web of a tent spider seems to him a puff of smoke in the grass, right there in the Luxembourg Gardens. He is amazed, she hears, at the gradual rise of matter into intelligence. He reveres that shift. Sharli brings him bread and pâté, cheese and celery, even though there is hardly room in his place for the two of them plus the bag of groceries. She tells him so, and then he vows to leave.

Instead, he tells her of new marvels. With your thin-beaked birds, he says, when the bird yawns or gapes, the sun on sunny days shines through the thin horn of it, and the yellow blazes.

And chambermaids, he says, always stand cakes of soap on their edges to drain them dry. No one likes a slimy soap. Hypersensitive people with colds, he tells her, insist on blowing their noses in peonies, and then she knows he is going too far, just being entertaining. She shakes her head in mild refusal.

He tries again, always, but only gets in deeper, claiming it is somehow godlike to foul up a perfect thing. Big wings whoosh over them, between them an engine idling, and it is as if they have been mesmerized from on high. They smile and kiss as it lands and rolls where the land slopes away. They have never seen a bad landing here, though many have been made. She is childlike and he is sublime. They do not need very much, even of each other. They go their separate ways.

He has never seen the kids she teaches. Only once has she seen him in the streets with his rat, but she has heard about him and cannot quite believe that Rat Man is hers, to cosset and nourish.

One day he will change, she knows. He has been constant for too long for him not to, but she has no idea how. He behaves young for imminent old age while she behaves rather solemnly for one so much younger than he. How she dreads that whiff of autumn coming off him. Not now, not yet, but hinted at in the sky of his eyes when his thoughts are especially rat-attuned and he remembers as if from an album of horrors a rotting shutter held fast by two rusted hinges, then a just as rusted sewing machine perched on the sill of an open window. The streets are full of greenish rubble and only the steps of the town are intact.

At this point the nightmare goes away. Or underground. There are no people, no animals. Nor is there stench or commotion. Embalming what he once upon a time saw, he has made it almost blank, but he knows if he goes to that town he must wear heavy leathers and a steel helmet. A church full of people burned, which included—he stops. In his case, it is the role of memory to go away. As if. No, no comparisons. Well, then, severe and beyond words. Something is hurting him. It has not worn off. The pain is a hardy perennial. It plucks at him. Its images come after him. Ironies like a nail file against his teeth. It is all very familiar. It orphans him.

I am one hundred and fifty-five today, he tells Sharli, but she adds the digits up to eleven and smiles the smile of rapt conspiracy.

This is his life. This is life, he thinks. You are dreaming again, Sharli tells him. You can hit the boulevards later. To the end of the runway they drive in her beat-up Citroën. They park, smoke, and cuddle as the heavy metal flies in over them, thundering and whining and droning. This is their fix, on the edge of the world. From time to time the police move them on, but they are doing no harm, whereas younger devotees lie on the grass beside the runway, with picnic baskets and sleeping bags.

Here they come again, she says. Did you ever see such rotten grins?

Is there a problem? the police ask.

We are choosing an airline, she tells them.

Park over there, the police say. And sit here.

But one day soon, she says, we too will be coming over this very spot. Our vacation. *He* needs one. Just look at him. The police do so and give up. Sharli smiles at their departing backs, and tells Rat Man he and she will fly over the end of the runway. It sounds as if she has said the end of the world, but he says nothing, murmuring assent. With their heads full of Paris, they will head for Menton. It doesn't matter where. Old place or new. Good place or bad. He would like to survive to see it. He talks to his heart, tells it to slow down. But it has a will of its own, running a race he knows little about. Try as she does, she cannot get him near a doctor's office. He does not do doctors.

He twists open the thermos and pours coffee for her, then for himself. A silver swan flows above them, tucking its legs neatly into its belly. No matter how many planes leave Paris, nothing of Paris ever goes away. Where is that nude Apollo with four horses with all the clouds and suns behind them? Wandering about, he retains things but fits them into a Paris in his head, not even divided up into districts. Where he could buy fantail pigeons, finches, parrots, parakeets, all in cages, he can also buy pickled lemons, couscous, roots of black horseradish, and goose sausage stuffed in a goose's neck. Crossing the small iron footbridge at the rear of Notre Dame, he reaches a quiet world of tree-shaded quays and snoozing courtyards, but also finds a striptease club in which Josephine Baker is still tossing bananas to the audience. His Paris is a scrambled one. Today still occupied by Nazis, tomorrow liberated, then occupied again. He will not wait for some official to accord him the freedom of the city. He has it already.

Even as she clasps his hand, he shudders, breaks into a sweat, takes a deep breath to calm his heart. If only everything did not excite him so. He huddles against her, breath still held, shaped like a chubby baboon, in a faded blue suit with silver blazer buttons, breathing wry discipline. All he needs, he knows, is some cause to rally to: not the cause of himself, but something outside of him that will magnify him just in time, before the hammerblow, the coup de grâce. It is bound to come. One does not wait in order merely to wait further. No destiny is like that. He will become a concierge at an illustrious hotel. Or custodian of some small collection, say the aquarium in the gardens of the Palais de Chaillot, dusting down an exhibit entitled River Fishes of France. He is not aiming high. He is not aiming at all. He is waiting to be aimed. Having worn his feet to shreds walking about Paris with an assortment of rats, or rat approximations, he can think of a thousand places where he might fit in. He would know what to do, except that his feet are not much use. Thickly callused, the soles are nearly numb, even when, after getting his shoes soaked through, he files them with a lump of pumice picked up he can't remember where. His objective is to erode the hardened skin, which otherwise splits and opens a crack deep into living tissue. He never manages to accomplish this, however. For days at a time he forgets to file, to rub, to scrape. The calluses build quiet as cement. And then crack.

One of his heavens to come, then, is to stand in glycerine, honey, a puddle of thick aloe juice.

Or to undergo perpetual chiropody in an establishment with gleaming chrome fixtures and fluffy white towels.

He wonders why an Almighty that can strike you dead would bother to humble you in so many small ways as well. Which proves the Almighty is not listening to reason or to tact. He longs for an Almighty more mediocre, less pedantic, not as thorough.

Like a cement mixer flung away by an explosion, a helicopter grinds over them. He shuffles his feet in his shoes now his breathing has slowed.

An ant roams across his thigh, up the inside of the window, then out.

He vows to read the newspapers again to see what the world is doing to itself. Something will show up. An event like a tidal wave. Just so long as it does not require a lot of walking. He is willing to stand, so he could become the liveried attendant who stands under a glass shelter amid the pink awnings of the Plaza-Athénée, the old hotel of Mata Hari.

What if it were snowing now? Would the planes still fly?

What if, out of the blue, so to speak, all the laws that permit flight broke down, along with acid's power to turn blue litmus paper red? (He remembers the facts, as well as the shocks, of his boyhood.) Then the wind would fly through the planes, after a suitable interval.

Sometimes he feels he is foaming.

Has turned liquid overnight.

And that Paris will blot him up never to be seen or hugged again. He needs the hugs more than he needs Paris. Sharli pays his gas bill too, although he is in general a man of the half-light, as willing to guess what the newsprint says as to turn up the gas to be sure. The sheath of threads which is the muslin mantle never burns bright.

Now they get out on the rough grass and begin their picnic on a blanket filched from some airline, whose monogram he burned away. Chopped grass blows against them, into their plastic wineglasses, onto their slab of pâté. As they munch and sip, a small airport truck bustles about, a platform for someone downing birds with a shotgun. Jets whine. The sun begins to fry his nose, so she attaches a slip of tissue to the bridge, moistened with spit and pâté, and then sees smuts from a chimney land on it. On the breeze, the faint strum of a double bass comes and goes, wafted toward them from the terminal.

No one, he thinks, could possibly forecast this experience in the round. It is unique.

Sharli watches him thinking this and relaxes, grateful that for once his mind is on something wholesome, something not of boulevard or rat.

When something flies over them, they stop chewing and part their mouths on the morsel. Then they resume, a little faster, touched by the thrill. People eating pâté are flying over two others also eating pâté. And flushing it with wine, a red Bordeaux from Pomerol.

But he is going nowhere today. It is enough to be near those who are. He holds his station under the flight path. Soothed by pâté, his soul fills with a strange light. He is a boy again, arranging the fox fur along a walking stick and alarming his parents by poking it round the edge of the salon door. They pretend to be surprised and shocked as the snout arrives and then the glossy neck in slow-motion flight, with not a sign of their son who, holding his breath, has trouble holding the stick steady. So the fox's head wobbles a bit as it slinks into full view.

Sniggers from behind the door.

He is peeping through the crack to watch their faces. Satisfied, he comes into view himself to amaze them. They are never unamazed. They dote on him and try to interest him in literature, but all he reads is guidebooks to Paris, while other boys move on to pornography. He is going to be a late developer, but at least when he does develop he will be different.

Years later, which is to say just now, he is talking to Sharli's thirteen-year-olds about his life on the boulevards, which sounds grand until he shrinks it and thins it out. Sharli has co-opted him, to get him out of himself, out of his box. A mailman, a taxi driver, a railroad conductor, a chef, and a concierge have preceded him in this course on civics. Some of them have been cantankerous, but they have all been paid.

She introduces him briefly, with no allusion to their personal lives, and he begins without the least trace of nervousness. Unaccustomed to public speaking, he does not even know what it is. Instead of talking about the rats, he gets into birds' beaks, Australian turtles, the way chambermaids drain soap, and then the dredging-up of warplanes. Prompted, he reveals the joys of parking under the takeoff point at the airport.

He cannot get into being a boulevardier, never mind how disreputable a one. She does not mind, and she lets him rumble on until he gets into it by accident, talking about himself as if he were not there as himself.

There is a man, he says, well known in his limited sphere, who walks the streets of Paris with a live rat under his coat. Not for money, but to wake people up.

He shows the students how, thrusting his hand under his not-tucked-in shirt and exposing it higher up, between the second and third buttons. It appears like a fin and they smile, they laugh aloud. He slides his hand back. They plead for more. The school principal looks in. Sharli half explains. The principal stares, then leaves. It was not his idea anyway, but decreed from above. Now his school is full of bums and layabouts. Never mind, the demonstration goes on. The children themselves make Rat Man motions. His explanation, bald as it is, interests them not at all. They enjoy the apparition, all the more when she produces the fox fur for him to maneuver with. He feels one acute pang, then gets on with it, wadding the fur under his shirt, then using a shawl she provides, in the end aligning the fox along a meter rule and coming round the edge of the doorway to show the kids what his own childhood was like.

Questions amaze him. Where did the rats come from? Were they white and trained? Was there any chance of disease or of being bitten? Did anyone try to buy a rat from him? Did the rats have names? Or numbers? Did he ever use baby rats? Was he frightened when he began? He answers all these, but the question that hovers in his own head is monstrous. Was there, it goes, another way of getting people's attention? An easier, more hygienic one? And, in the case of the fox, one less poignant. Terrible things happened to this Rat Man's parents, he says, lapsing into the impersonal again. He became an orphan. Are any of them orphans? Two hands rise. A tear forms and bulges. Rat Man wipes it away and drives ahead. All that remained, he says, was a doll's house and a fox fur. Really, he decides right there in front of them, he should have borne the doll's house through the streets as an affliction. The money would have poured in. Even if they didn't believe him. The rat, the fur, was just a reminder of a reminder.

None of this goes into what he tells them. Now he is into the technique of it. How to expose the snout, how to make it seem to move, how to tug it out of sight and have to wrestle with it under one or two layers of clothing. Sometimes, he tells them, straying far afield, when you enter a supermarket and select a cart at random, it begins to misbehave and you have to wrestle it with all your might just to keep all four wheels on the floor. It wants to go speeding away on two wheels like those cars in the movies. That done, he resumes his outdoor career, saying it in the first person.

Don't you ever get tired of it? The voice comes from a distance.

Tired of it now, he answers by remote control. Something else will come along soon, if not true splendor, then a regular position at some hotel. He had once thought of becoming a travel agent, but no more. All the interesting travel has been done. The world is too much traveled as it is.

This puzzles them. Are there no unknown places?

Not on this planet, he answers. The travel agent of the future will have to discover ways of keeping people at home. Travel will be done through little kits of sounds and smells, blades of grass and feathers from the region's birds. There will be too many people at every destination. No one will be allowed to move. The longest journey will be to the cemetery.

Sharli intervenes, thanks him formally, and the applause is sustained. A plumber will follow him next week, and then an air hostess. Book learning dies a natural death in the presence of raw lives, and she does not mind. But Rat Man has done his hour, much more than she expected. He might have clammed up altogether or just waggled the fox fur at them. They will remember him when other visitors have faded into oblivion. He will haunt them as one of the outcast, one of the not quite right in the head. An original. One of the unnumbered. A mutant. And perhaps, in later years, some of these children will head for the boulevards to find him, plying his dismal trade among the wits and the rubberneckers. He may be there, but it is doubtful. He will have gone on to UNESCO, or things even bigger, having served his sentence and sipped his joys. Of today, at any rate, he's had enough.

He makes his own way home, gets in by pushing against the top of the door that supposedly opens outward only from within, and sighs with relief. He likes that door, swinging as it does vertically, though few have pounded on it to get at him. With weary finesse, he ruffles some cotton between his fingers, wets it a bit to make a couple of points, then lifts the roof of the doll's house and sets the wool in one of the empty bedroom chairs.

Sometimes I behave, he concludes, as if I was never born but assembled bit by bit in a garden shed. I crept around the door of life and will similarly creep out. Unless something magnificent detains me.

Four

Out into the tiny street he goes to rummage for something to toy with. He finds an old frayed tape measure and wraps it around his thumb like a bandage, all of a sudden captivated by the idea of living every instant like this: using to the maximum whatever comes to hand. And no cheating. No fudging. Nothing prearranged.

What else is here, then, to challenge him? An empty book of matches, which he peels into shreds, almost making from it a flat flower.

A worn-down toothbrush catches his eye, cached in a banana skin, and he brushes his fingernails with it, wondering about whose teeth the bristles have stroked in, oh, this must be a five-year-old brush. The roots of the tufts are black. Now he decides to keep it to brush the floors of the doll's house.

And that does it, sets off the awfulness all over again. It comes in spates. He hears young men singing, drunken singing in what he knows is German. It is all around him.

Together with this noise of overgrown, boisterous children comes an evocative smell of roast beef ready for the table. It might be Sunday.

His mind shifts to the locked-up ruins enclosed by a low wall. Three gates. One sign says *Remember,* another *Silence.* A few postcards gleam on sale at a modest kiosk. This is where it happened, although, he tells himself, much more of it happened in his head. He was there.

Now he is again on the site, although he has not gone there since he was twenty-five or so. He dips a boy's toe into the tramline track and slides it forward in the groove as if it were a wheel. These have survived intact, but the buckled bicycles have not, nor the coffee grinders, the saucepans, the bird-busy hulk of the village doctor's car.

Plastic or china flowers catch his eye.

A plain headstone with the passport photograph of an attractive girl embossed into it sends him to the caption beneath. He thinks he knew her, but by now he thinks he has known everyone.

He views the sites of the worst happenings: the smithy, the barns, the bakery, the church, and farmyard wells, the two-seat outdoor privies.

There is almost nowhere, he decides, that will not accommodate an act of abomination without the slightest protest. No chunk of wood or metal says wait a minute, you mustn't do that.

Ici, says another sign: *Here.* It happened *here,* right where you are standing, as well as in a million other places of which local indignation takes no heed. He remembers erratically how it was at the time, when he hid in the hazel bushes after his parents first hid him under the floorboards.

That *then* is a blur installed in ragged memories of visits to the site, and these memories do not come together in one clinched image he might call My Memory of It. My Recollection. If they ever do, enabling him to relive it all in one second, his heart will burst, his head will turn into a flare.

So: dribs, drabs. He lives, and this is his phrase for how, at only three-quarter rat power. Forty years after, with Sharli mothering and fathering him according to his fatigued needs, he still has not put it all together. He keeps the ingredients of a deadly formula apart.

A rusted bath in a roofless bathroom? Yes. It is now full of rain.

In the church, before the altar, a smashed baby cart? Yes. It cannot be wheeled away, but only dragged. It stays put, to warn.

What then of the molten bells? Sharli has tried hard to make him accept their silence as an homage to the dead. Their unringability is a blessing, she says; but he always liked their sound, festive and busy and gently otherworldly.

What then of the bakery ovens? What was in *them?* Sharli will not help him deal with that, but he seems to recall a sign that read *Deux corps calcinés.* His mind goes away from that toward little model people made of bread and baked by the baker as a joke.

Yet, he adds, someone spray-painted *Forget* (though not *Forgive)* on all the signs that said *Remember.* Why would anyone do that, even a German tourist? The new village is just lumps of boring concrete, a blind bureaucrat's substitute although given the same name as the old village that remains a relic.

Yet in that new village, like something put together from a child's brand-new building set, the oldest survivor lives: Madame R., woman in a steely hairnet, with a clothespin in her mouth to keep her lips from quivering. She pushed through a church window and that was that.

Was it she whom they forced at gunpoint to make omelettes for them? Even, perhaps, while he ran the seven kilometers and lost a shoe?

And did she, after it was all over, join the burial parties and walk through the remains of the village wearing, like all of them, a handkerchief soaked in eucalyptus against the smell? They must have looked like outlaws from a Western movie.

Red Cross workers helped by young seminarists were the salvage teams. With long rubber gloves and, yes, the handkerchiefs, at neither of which he can look without sensing a new disaster.

One letter they found, though stained with blood, read: "I am quite well at the present and enjoying the sunshine."

Plus lipstick holders.

Corset stiffeners.

Belt buckles.

Powder compacts.

And those two mirror images: the page from an exercise book, bearing a solitary sentence, and then the blackboard it was copied from: *Je prends la résolution de ne jamais faire de mal aux autres.* I resolve never to do others harm.

Two crucifixes, both unscathed, one of wood, the other resilvered.

In one barn, the remains of thirty sheep no doubt used for target practice.

All the cats had survived, huddled together in one house, yowling to be fed.

He hears them, the hens and rabbits milling wildly about, the swallows soaring in search of their lost nests, but he does not link them up. He never gets much past this point. After Monsieur P., owner of the local garage, dead halfway through a fence with a live horse tethered to his arm and munching grass, he never goes far at all.

It is far away, he tells himself, as far as Paris from the Middle Ages, the Dark Ages, the Age of Stone. In the age of jet travel, the Stone Age is traveling away from him at almost the speed of light. It must. Yet it seems also only just around the edge of tomorrow.

Outside a certain circumference, the houses went untouched. Who, then, drew the circle? Who stabbed the village center with the almighty needle while the marker scribed the radius of death?

Well within it, he ran well beyond it, almost into the next massacre, if there had been one. It used to be one of his four or five jokes, wan and mysterious. He uses it no more. He is beyond jokes. You don't *tell* them, he says, you turn *into* one, and Sharli scoffs, hushes him for getting melodramatic, and lays a folded wet facecloth on his wrists, the back of his neck, and his brow. Up he climbs onto his shelf. His eyes close.

Now he longs for his winter outfit: belted raincoat, silk scarf, the old hat called a trilby, and his collar turned up high. A figure both sinister and traditional, he is truly anonymous in such attire: George Raft, with a touch of Bogart and of Eddie Constantine. Very much of the movies, but not when he murmurs (he murmurs this maybe once a year now, if that): Americans are happier when being addressed by a millionaire, or a multimillionaire; it makes them feel in touch with what matters.

Sometimes he murmurs such things into the bushes in the Luxembourg, coyly plucking white hairs from his wrist (or, in summer, his exposed chest) and fingertipping them into the leaves, the grass. They do not want to leave him, though. They cling. They will not brook this last severance. Even his hair loves him. Well, it should, he decides, after all we've been through, after the war, the peace, and all those other indeterminate times, eras even, that seem to be no more one thing than another. The messy, blurred chunks of mere waiting. Down he clambers, to the doll's house. Off with the roof.

He sees the same spider in the same corner, having countless times crouched in front of it, half inclined to kill it with a poke of his finger.

Too intimate, that.

Well, then, with the end of a pencil or a rolled-up piece of newspaper the same diameter.

Yet it devours ants, mosquitoes, flies; and, tiny as it is,

serves him as charwoman. Someone more imaginative than he would by now have named it and staged imaginary conversations with it, making an indoor cult of the thing, trapping ants, mosquitoes, flies, to plant in its web just as gently as he plants his white hairs in the Luxembourg.

He refers less to days of the week (Sunday, Monday, and so forth) than to days of rain, snow, wind, hail, frost, heat humid or dry. As a result, with all types of weather taken into account, he ends up with some ten types of days, although only two or three of them happen in any given week, such is the monotony of weather.

He groups things thus, much as he groups his memories: all cut throats are one, all broken legs, all heavy boxes of explosive with long white fuses trailing out of them like roots.

Such a habit saves him, literally, from himself; he is one among many. But he does not recall, except in outline, what happened after the village was burned. In fact, for several years, Madame R., one of the few escapees, took him in and brought him up. This was the childhood he never wanted, was obliged to have. He has erased it. He has made it erase itself. The hands that smell of cauliflower and cumin do not exist. Her loud voice, almost that of a Great Dane, does not sound in his head. Nor the quiet shove with which nightly she forced him into sleep, pushing his head from the forehead down into the pillow that had no case.

Yet, glory be, she it was who, singing the "Marseillaise" with a loud, nasal, almost drumlike emphasis, dipped her hands into the ruins of the house he grew up in and somehow found the doll's house, the fox fur, and a few other odds and ends.

Had he asked her to find them? Or had she done it unprompted, knowing a boy like this must surely have a doll's house in the house somewhere? But why a girl's toy? A mother's fox fur made sense; he would surely want it, and she would surely have had one. But a doll's house? Was there, somewhere in the ruins of the house, a sister he had never seen? Kept in the attic because terrible to look at? Or was he, as a boy, girlish? No, it was the mother's, from the first years of the century, so the doll's house and the fox fur spanned her life from girlhood into womanhood. A pipe of his father's would have helped, but his father must have had the favorite one with him when he last left the house.

Did all these things reek of smoke? Poussif spent hours *thinking* the smoke away from them, much as (maybe) Madame R. hosed the smoke off him.

He remembers the weather without the people with which it has been involved.

If he played as a growing boy, it was in limbo. The jerseys, the shorts, the hoops, the bow and arrow, have gone. Perhaps there were other children living with Madame R. in her two-up, two-down cottage in the next village. If so, he remembers them neither from school nor from at home round the stewpot in the evenings, or dunking crust in hot chocolate at dawn.

Instead, he dimly sees himself stooping in order to pass under something while, at the same time, stepping high in order to go over something else. An incongruous movement, this, it affects his gait when he launches himself into the street: head lowered, knees lifted. As a boy, perhaps, he listened a great deal at keyholes, blew into them, or peered. He has had to pass over many bodies in order to keep going.

Walk upright, Sharli says. Be taller.

He tries, but as his head rises the knee comes after it.

And then, as the knee descends, his head begins to droop again.

He can do only half of it. Something invisible blocks his path, and he always seems to be ducking, feinting, getting out of the line of fire.

Saying as little as he does (except when addressing her class at school on a formal occasion), he nonetheless comes out with things that amaze her with their weight and delicate profundity. On one occasion, no doubt in response to some echo from childhood, when being babied although too old for that, he told her that, if everything in the world were truly small, people would be able to talk in diminutives without ever causing embarrassment. Shar*lette,* he grins, going on to Sharlettina and Sharlettinettina, which he can hardly say.

I don't mind, she says, but it sounds like a disease: *scarlatine.*

In *my* day, he tells her, evoking the Dark Ages, people actually caught it and were taken away wrapped in a scarlet blanket. He thinks the part about the blanket is true. If not, it should be.

Then he tries to tell her something he never quite gets into the open. After the church has burned, its tower remains intact, although you can see right through it now, it has no insides. The thing transports him back to an age of cannibalism and unspeakable savagery that have no place in world history. Ogres eat coal. Dinosaurs pound saber-toothed tigers. Mammoths learn to swim in sludge, a meter a week. Flowers abound, but they are all poisonous. Gigantic crevasses split the surface of the planet and thousands of beings fall into them howling. The weather changes from hour to hour. It snows through unbearable heat and the snow falls only half down. The rest falls as hot rain. Things grow at speed, engulfing the Neanderthals where they crouch. There will never be a world for humans to inhabit. He traces the demise of humankind along a dead-end tangent of his own devising. Evolution takes an unhistorical turn and that is that. He is alone, in his room, among the sponges. No rats, no Sharli, no Nazis, only the gamut of enormous weather invisible to Sharli, but present when he oversteps a drift of indoor snow, shields his head with several newspapers from rain scalding or almost sleet, and hides his head and eyes to keep the desert wind away. This is not his act, or any series of acts, but the metaphor he lives by. It somehow relates his hovel to prehistory, to the innocence of a planet whose only attribute to that point happens to be a climate. Too much horror at an early age, he tells her, and you never respond to it again. Responding is worse than being callous.

So she plays along, accepting it when he says his room is full of driftwood, or mold exactly on the point of turning to coal. She helps him wrestle the big storks that occupy every available inch, or the anacondas that devour his newspapers. She scolds the in-room glacier for going too slow and pets the enormous rat that guards the doll's house. Such behavior, on his part, is no stranger than what he used to do, sitting in the places reserved for *mutilés de guerre* in the Métro and refusing to budge. Somewhere, drafted after the umpteenth scene with the gendarmerie, she has the official letter which explains why he must be left alone: This man is psychologically wounded. As soon as he got the letter, he stopped trying to sit among the *mutilés,* weirdly convinced that he was now among the sane and whole. The letter freed him. It gave him the freedom of the city. It promoted him to an even higher plane of non-belonging. There was more of life into which he did not fit.

Yet this saddened him not at all, not when compared to the fates of others, including those whose punishment he imagined as being obliged to say aloud numbers so long, indeed so interminable, that the poor swine were still mumbling them in panic on their deathbeds, their death rattle a spew of unrelated digits, their tongues continuing after their brains left off. No form of abbreviation was allowed them. Nothing raised to such and such a power. It was the long-winded enumeration of the universe, akin in his mind to saying aloud the whole of the Code Napoléon or the Paris telephone book, rather than referring to them by name. He delighted to think how much this would slow civilization down. Even the murdered, the burned, would be murdered and burned that much more slowly, especially if the Nazi or generalized Hun in question had to reel off one by one each and every atom of the victim before getting to work.

Before setting fire to a church, recite its entire history.

And the pedigree of horses, dogs, and hens.

And, before the at-gunpoint making of omelettes for the riotous soldiery (some of them mere boys inflamed with *vin ordinaire,* to which they were not accustomed), the exquisitely accurate description of an egg's molecular structure, and how in the omelette it changes.

Yet, in a world going ever so slowly backwards, even to advance at a snail's pace made him too fast, so, for a while anyway, he tried to go slower than usual, taking several minutes to produce the rat from within his coat.

Too long, they cried. *We have to go.*

They offered him money and wine if only he would hurry up. They mimicked his motions, pretending to bring the rat from within their own coats, or up from between their breasts. He never wavered, though, intent upon the slowness of his rat delivery, and dimly aware of some principle of showmanship that said: If the audience knows the outcome, then the core of the act is its execution. If the outcome, or denouement, is famous, then hone the presentation for all you're worth. So, every twitch, feint, shove, mattered enormously. Certainly Rat Man has had imitators, but they were crude yokels compared to him, who performed his piece as if confronting the watchers with several thousand frames from a movie epic to be called *Rat Man of Paris.*

That was then, since when he has speeded up, although never what you would call swift.

Put it this way. There was a time when his world shrank, and he almost came to a mental halt within it, allowing Madame R. once a week to strip him in a nearby barn and hose him down. If for any cause his penis stiffened during this ablution, she tapped it down with a flick of her cane. There was another time, however, mainly after meeting Sharli, when his life broadened out, and then he began to go at the speed of other people, except that several times a week he yearned for that other, golden time when he might humbly set a cauliflower on the doorstep of someone who had been kind to him. Even in bad weather he would take half an hour over this, in the act recalling the farmer's field he had stolen it from, the farmer's face, the farmer's dog, and then fondling the soft spotty face of the white part, the rubbery green of the leaves. And then, of course, he visualized the face of the recipient. He usually left whatever he stole under cover of darkness, which was when he stole it too. Never a truffle, though; he had no pig to help him. But almost anything else, including grapes. He came from a country region and he cherished country ways.

In short, as far as *delivery* went, of rat or booty, he was always a bit of a slow coach, and he got away with it because people indulged him as a loony. Now, he still puzzles Sharli when he visits her and pointedly averts his gaze from the TV set, or turns his back on it, but only if she has switched it on.

Not far from the end of the runway where they go and sit together to be thoughtless, a small herd of deer come out of the woods in the evening to crop clover, and these he loves to watch, sometimes letting out an uncouth-sounding whistle, which only makes them tilt their heads and flash their tails. What amazes him is that, so far, no one has stolen them, shot them with bow and arrow, or frightened them away. Perhaps, he reasons to her, they are stone-deaf from the aero-engines thundering above them when they are out of sight. He is not sure. A sign on the runway warns pilots about the local deer, but no sign on the greensward warns deer about aircraft. It seems a one-way deal to him: if only the deer were larger, with hundreds of horsepower, and the planes smaller, the size of deer, say, then things would be nobler.

One day soon, he will turn his attention to other things. Pot plants by the thousand for a market gardener who will pay him handsomely.

Unless something better turns up: some call to the colors, an assignment to the Foreign Legion, an invitation to be shepherd to the deer. Deerherd, he thinks. Are there any such anymore? Were there ever any? For the present, he waits in the quiet swill of his awful and pleasant memories, feeling his dues to society were paid long ago when he was a boy hiding in the hazel bushes with his cap and satchel. Sharli bathes him; no one hoses him down. Sharli feeds him and smilingly schools his maladroit sexual overtures. He shows no finesse, but then, sexually, he is a mere eighteen, and all he has is headlong vigor. Things will improve. She knows that. It is a tacit promise extorted from history.

She cuts his hair, his nails, cleans out the sharp whiteheads of his shaving rash, and pops the pimples on his back. Even in middle age, his hormones have still not settled down. To her, he is another of her pupils: bigger, heavier, and more of a liability, to be sure, yet a fount of promise so long as he is able to take his time. She doubts if his big day will ever arrive: the call to the colors, the Foreign Legion, the herd of deer; he does not have the right connections for any of that. In fact, he has almost no connections at all. She is content, having found him, to tend him as he blooms in going down (her own phrase, to herself, for his prospects); as he comes into his own while getting old; as he soars into maturity in his sixties, a greenhorn emeritus.

Never mind, she tells him: trapped field mice have worn their fur away trying to get out of a cage. All you have to do is learn to breathe as if all the air in the world belonged to you.

Only my portion, he answers.

If you took more than your fair share, she tells him, you'd be depriving nobody of theirs.

Amazing, he says, how much of it there is. Always the right gas to keep us going.

No, she tells him. What is amazing is that it was there, so we could be here. We came into being because there was air, and then the air stayed put. That's what I call destiny.

He inhales deeply, nodding, tries to keep two lungfuls to himself, but has to let it out in a gasping sigh. With both hands she appears to seize its volume, squeeze it into a coconut shape, and hand it back to him. That's for plants, she says, knowing that he has never quite trusted plants indoors, believing contrary to fact that they give off noxious fumes. Now he agrees with her, but he has never quite rid himself of suspicion, or of his haste to hide cutlery during thunderstorms.

Five

Something meticulous in him almost drives her mad. He fusses about a stamp's being stuck straight on its envelope, parallel to both corners. If she stacks dishes, he has to remake the stack into a minaret with the smallest on top. It's logical, he says, but she tells him he'd like it that way even if it weren't. She has a habit of folding the phone book over and then leaving the phone half on the spine's bulge, half on the tilted page, and this troubles him a lot. The world is a terrifying, mesmerizing mess, and he needs his grids to keep it straight, keep it at bay.

On the other hand, when he gets to work in her tiny patio two meters square, his finicky ways pay off. Within the main square is a smaller one in which there grows a hawthorn tree surrounded at its base by white marble chips relieved by tinted stones, bits of shiny coal, and shells from the seashore. Fallen leaves obscure much of this display, so every so often he kneels down and puffs the leaves away or brushes them gently off with a soft-bristled hearth brush. Then he picks off by hand the colored stones, smooths out the area with both hands, and pours onto it the bag of new chips she provides. He maneuvers the heap of chips almost as if kneading dough, with a touch of primitive reverence. As if the chips were of his own making. That done, he replaces the stones, sometimes actually choosing positions for them, at other times tossing a handful down to see where they will fall. Either way, the effect seems to please him, and she notes how, at least once during each cleanup, he goes inert with his hands plunged into the depth of the marble chips. Stranded in time, he lets the chips talk to his head through his gritty palms, as much a god incognito (she thinks), fondling the atoms of a creation absentmindedly made, as a handyman doing a simple chore with his mind on something else—bananas, weather, the orange smear an eraser leaves behind it. Not that he writes things down much, but he longs for an eraser that will wipe things clean.

Then he replaces the bits of driftwood which complete this little petrified oasis, and straightens up, rubbing his knees with a grimace. She had never noticed it until he pointed it out: one of the driftwood branches has a gargoyle face in its contours when the sun strikes it a certain angle: a face both taut and bothered, with long tuber nose and heroic set to the mouth.

Me, he says. *Voilà.*

Your own face is fatter, she tells him.

Then I will diet until I fit, he says. It's a hint from nature as to how I ought to look.

She nods, then admires his work, amazed that the century still can include a man who removes leaves and dandelions one by one, then scoops them all into a heap he brushes into a paper bag moistened so that its lips will hug the patio stone.

He is not always so fastidious, though, having once taken the initiative without counting the cost. He sprayed an entire hornets' nest with shaving foam, stung by the sentries but persisting until he had in front of him an asteroid of cream, through whose curd bedraggled hornets slid with wet wings. In a sense, what he did worked, but, after the foam dried and withered, hornets filled the tiny courtyard, drunk on lather, glycerine, propane, or whatever, and refused to go back in.

Wiser now, he still looks at the branch where the nest was, and he smiles the smile of Maréchal Foch: not until he is surrounded and out of ammunition will he attack in earnest.

At other times, for her, he adjusts the little rug that daily "creeps" toward the fireplace, only three centimeters a day, but enough to make him uneasy when it is underfoot. He likes to see a clear narrow space between the rug and the fireplace. He is the maestro of the spaces in between things, the angles which unnoticed things make when intersecting one another. In his time a great watcher of the horizon, he remembers his first response to its actual curve. Indignation, awe, disappointment, all came into it. He had heard these things were so, and here was the meniscus bulging away from him, parallel with nothing at all. Here it is, every day, like a mirage. He would like to will it straight.

At first sight a fussbudget, he comes closer to being a connoisseur of life's neglected corners, its always wasted little chances. At one extreme of trifling tenderness he lifts up the wicker wastebasket in her bathroom (the one she moves to a dry zone each time she bathes) and appraises it for volume and diameter, envisioning the exact size of paper bag that will fit. After rummaging in a cupboard, where market bags lie folded flat, he taps the bag open to its full capacity, almost like a metalsmith removing dents, and rolls down the lip, all around, until the bag is just the right depth for the basket. That done, he smooths the rolled paper flat and carefully fits it inside, patting it flush with the curved interior. The coarse noisy paper never sits quite flush despite his working on it with both palms, but the result delights her every time; the choked bag of before has gone when she returns from school or shopping, and the basket is immaculate for use again: lined, neat, and trim. The bag has become the basket's, whereas, usually, when she does the job herself it is the bag that somehow blots out the basket, towering above it, billowing, inviting her to throw it away empty. With Rat Man around, however, she need not worry. He notices what civilization ignores. An amorist of bits and bobs, he might, if he had been otherwise schooled by Madame R., have become an authority on how Charlemagne brushed his teeth, on the sounds Napoleon made when he sat alone to have a good think, on the hairs in Captain Dreyfus' nose. Instead, here comes Madame R., that canny disciplinarian, tying him to an iron bed for three days while she goes away, commanding him not to mess himself. Or else. The most he ever did was wet himself, and that dried up. Then he spent hours trying to iron the mildly yellowed sheet with his round rear end, so that it would seem flat when she returned. It was always the same. Back she bustled, and she always hosed him down, yelling abuse as if the Germans had never done enough, to him, to her, to them.

Cleanliness, Madame R. tells him from a thousand meters away. *Cleanliness—*

Cannot be achieved, ever, he tells himself in his mind. It went out with the Chinese water torture.

One day you will manage it, my boy.

And I will be in a winding sheet. He feels free to weep under the bombardment from her hose. Is it really she in rubber gloves who rubs his face in the wet bed? Who sits him on the chamber pot and commands him to empty himself of a liter? Who makes him wear wet pajamas under his school clothes? Waves a neatly folded oilcloth at him and roars? He cannot win. Afraid to mess the grand old family bed, he wets the brand-new rug on the floor. Clearly, Madame R. says, he is unaccustomed to living in a civilized place. By summer, she has banished him to a camp bed in the milk house, where he has severe, incomplete dreams, in one seeing the entire continent of India moving northward a thumb's length each year. He has never needed India before, but now he is afraid it will vanish during his sleep next week or the week after, and all through this time of his life he cannot even persuade himself that, at such a rate, India will remain in view, unlosable and vast. Where could it go? One day soon, in France or India, he tells himself, he will hose down Madame R., probing *her* most secret places with a wand of water, and then rope her too upon an iron bed, rub her face in it, brandish an oilcloth at her, commanding her to be as clean as May. *Now,* he wonders: Why clean as May? Where did that come from? What's clean about it? It must be the tiny laundry of the blossom out to dry.

Worst of all, she sometimes makes him watch when she squeezes the sores around her ankles, or, when she is angered beyond measure, makes him do it for her, with hot bread poultices that make her yell with pain and send her into an even fiercer rage. As she pushed through that window to escape, the flames licked her feet and legs. She got out, not unscathed, but all he can think of is the broken glass and how she somehow did not gash herself. Maybe her face and trunk heal faster than her legs. Her shoes, he knows, saved her feet. Out she shot, her tail aflame, a Joan of Arc *manqué,* ready to make the world pay—for saving her or depriving her of martyrdom, he can never be sure.

Whenever he dreams back, it is always Sharli untying him from that bed, then soaping him down in the bath (after removing the wicker basket to a safe place by the door). The impossible he does not mind, it is the possible that scares him, because, deep down, he is on the side of paralysis. When something threatens to happen, he dodges aside, scoots away mentally, until the threat subsides. One day she catches him in the kitchen, trying to force toothpaste from a jumbo tube into a tiny giveaway size: one nozzle against the other. Or so it looks until she sees that the smaller nozzle is actually inside the other one. The fit is neat, but the toothpaste is not moving, never mind how hard Rat Man squeezes.

The air, she tells him, has no way of getting out. It has to escape before the toothpaste can move in.

Damn the air, he murmurs. I thought I was doing all the good in the world.

Open one end, then crimp it shut.

That would be cheating, he answers, his face all forlorn gravity.

The force in the metal, she instructs him, is greater than the force with which you push the paste from one tube to the other. And then there is the matter of the air. None of it will ever work.

Almost in a fury, he sets down both tubes and motions her to cap them. I was trying to save you weight, he says. You shouldn't have to carry the big one to school. The little one was empty. You like your mouth to feel fresh. You have a right not to have to buy another sample size. Everyone has, if they've bought the jumbo.

If the nozzles were less tight a fit, she begins. Then she gives up. His remorseless attention to detail, coupled with his disdain of general principles, drives her to the brink. And yet he means so well, trying to adapt the world to her needs, to make a nest from a handful of prickly hay. Because, she decides, his attention to detail hasn't made of him a scientist, which in another age it might, it leads him astray, into—into what? Options no one has ever bothered with, now or ever. A sheep might seem more like blotting paper to him. Like that. A broom has a haircut. Yes. He will think of a cup as a container for toes, ten at a time. He *is* original, I know, but so original he doesn't belong anywhere. He doesn't have anything in common with anybody, and this makes him a sort of mental orphan, except he's too big, a sort of outcast, except he's sometimes a quite convincing human being, a sort of

Phantom of the Opera, except he's very physical at times and the opera would have no lyrics. Once you get used to him, you're sunk. The thing to have done, before getting used to him, would have been to pass him by.

Six

Months later, over jasmine blossom tea and petits fours, on a rainy day, he is showing her his most recent newspaper clipping, which, for once, he is going to fasten to the empty line in his little hovel. Something from Trenton, New Jersey, has found its way to Paris, no doubt marred in both transit and translation, but enough to excite him. He shows her the canister of salt substitute she bought months ago and taps his finger at the chemical called potassium chloride.

Instead of salt, she says. It's safer.

It's deadlier, he says. In New Jersey, at the Trenton State Prison, they are going to execute the condemned by injecting them in a vein. He reads aloud, with courtly disdain:

Three syringes, three drugs: thiopental sodium, which causes unconsciousness; pancuronium bromide, which paralyzes the lungs; and *potassium chloride,* which produces abnormal heart rhythms and eventual heart failure. How would you like your heart to fail like that of one of the New Jersey murderers? She drops the teapot on the table, not breaking it, but spilling the tea. Aghast, she reads it, believes it, and lets the spilled tea lie where it fell.

Would they really do that to anyone? she asks in a stunned, ruminative tone.

It is one of the last remaining human privileges, he tells her. When there are so many things we can't do, it's one of the things we can. It makes things tidy. It's tidiness itself. It's a cleanser.

She stares at him gently, telling herself: Well, what did you expect? Ever since what happened to him as a child, the aromas of cooking have made him sick. One of his great ambitions is to become a decoy carver specializing in ducks. He reminds me of the coelacanth, who, after millions of years undetected in the deep ocean, lumbers up into the light and gets caught. A specimen. He is entitled. Holding hands out at the end of the runway, he remembers everything. Nothing escapes him. It was he who told me that the graveyards adjoining the harvest fields are full. Now the graves are beginning to invade the crops. The dead are nourishing the crops. He liked that idea. It made the world a bit smaller for him. More manageable. Big suffering and little compensations. That's his style. He has a vested interest in ways into and out of the world. Being in the world is the slightest thing to him. A penance. A fluke, a mishap. It's what's on either side that wins his interest. He doesn't ask much, but he knows a lot. That's it. I'm dumb. He long ago found out what most of us spend a lifetime shrinking from.

Well, she says, that's New Jersey for you. I personally wouldn't want to go farther than the Channel Islands. Old Jersey. Nothing like that goes on there.

Wait, he whispers. They'll all have to come to it sooner or later. There's a human tide. We can't keep installing the murderers in little colleges for life, doubling and tripling them up in one cell. Now and then, the herd has to be culled. Just to make a human space again. In which something good might happen. Room for someone nice. You have to give the innocent a chance to spread themselves.

For him this is talkative. She smiles at the thought, reminding herself that, had it not been for what happened to him what seems a lifetime ago, he might never have noticed the evil that infests the planet. She tells him so.

Then I'd be lucky, he says. It would be like walking without ever seeing the sky. Without ever knowing it was up there, ready to fall. All emptied out. As if an ocean had been removed and there was nothing left save that big blue bedsheet and its fluff. Its fleece. Yes, it's the fleece that makes you notice it. If there were clear skies for ever and ever, I think we'd all walk around just looking down. Very glum. Heaven would be underground.

She chortles. Maybe it is!

He corrects her in the mildest way he has, which is to say with a cockeyed smile and a hand against her forehead, erasing the error through pressure. It is more likely, he says, to be found in the vicinity of the large luxury hotels under the porte cochère, in a small forgotten cardboard box awaiting delivery by a blind man from the Middle Ages.

Sharli is willing to let that stand as one of the articles of his faith. There is no arguing with him; he has to be coaxed into saying anything at all connected, so there is no point in weighing his images. What he comes up with floats him to the surface, from wherever the bulk of his being lurks.

Now he informs her that, since coming upon the news item about death in New Jersey, he is going to try to keep up to date. More newspapers. Newer ones at the window of his bolthole. The world is full of marvels, even now. He wants to keep up with it. A sort of at-arm's-length relationship with catastrophe.

Knowing how much he can make from how little, she

makes a mental note to supply him with a few extra clippings a week. Yet, she wonders, should she be in a position of choosing and sifting what he gets to brood about? Custodian of a ghost, must she be his censor too? Or trust to chance? To guide is also to compel. Yet to keep hands off is to risk everything.

How, she asks herself, can she be so tentative with him when, at times, he knows exactly how to deal with her? When she can't sleep, because her feet and calves are full of unwanted motion, maybe the unspent lower energy of a day spent sitting down, he counsels her to wriggle all her toes and her ankles until they refuse to move. Then she will sleep. She does. Her toes exhaust themselves, the calves and ankle joints too. But there is no similar way of stilling him. He has few signs of life. His pulsing name belies him. He coasts through history. He browses on the grasslands of time. Nothing detains him much. He floats, he roams, he tunes himself in and out, one of the most—she gropes for the word—*dispersed* humans since . . . whoever. She grins. The worry is over. To take him seriously does not mean she has to be all solemn about him.

A walk, she suggests.

Where are we?

Latitude and longitude? Like that?

No, he answers. I was thinking of the year. Whereabouts are we in the year? Where in time? I see leaves, but can I trust it to be autumn? I still feel hot. I always do. It's always red-hot summer under my jaw.

Once upon a time she suspected his natural body temperature was half a degree too high, and persuaded him to let her apply a thermometer. On that day, his temperature was low, and this fact made him merry, at least in his awkward way of being so: a big blink, a croupy cough, a hand waved high as if to bat away all the words that could not describe how enlivened he felt.

Everyone has quirks, she told him. You're like everyone else. In that.

At that she began to talk carefully, realizing how close the heat under his jaw (about which he regularly complains even in winter) was to the inferno of all the villagers burned alive in the church. Only her book of gargoyles soothes him. They look cool, he says. As she turns the pages, hearing the expensive paper rattle and flex, she hands him cookies from a tin. At one demented, twisted face in half a dozen, he exclaims, puffing crumbs, and points: *Rat Man is awake,* he cries, delighted by anyone as ugly as he. Or as ugly as he thinks he is. On good days, though, he tends to think he has a face both seemly and young, a touch of Charles Boyer going to seed. But she never demurs. She smiles a gratified smile when he cries the cry of self-recognition. It is as if, backhandedly, the world has noticed him, has lifted him ever so gently from within the folds of long-forgotten history. The smile and the cry are those of a ten-year-old, and at these times she feels more mother than nurse, certainly more nurse than beloved, but without doubt more beloved than foolish.

So: she has ways of both energizing him and soothing him. That his response to either stimulus is primitive, childlike, or even mindless, bothers her not a jot. She tames him, sorts him out, gets his keel even, until he is ready for yet another sortie along the boulevards, with Sharli following at a distance, a witness to prove to him he is real. That, with his funny walk, he is having a life at all.

II

An Almost Invisible Number

Seven

He never turns around to look at her, but, from time to time, with one hand behind him, he curls his little finger in discreet hello. The finger is the tiny hook that holds her to him as he (at least in his mind's eye afterwards) barges through the crowds, looms at the tables, gains his effect, and, half tumbling, half hovering, moves from site to site, a tourist draw. Immersed thus in people, he at last feels a member of something other than the order of excluded beings.

Then he tells her that, over the past few weeks, a little Spanish novelist in exile has begun to follow him about, taking notes. A thin, dark, hook-nosed fellow, he tells her, like a flame you want to cup your hand around to shield him from the wind. Juan Madero, he thinks. Or is it José?

How, she has to ask it, do you know? Spanish? Novelist? I would have seen him.

He walks behind *you*. José Menéndez. Or Juan. A name like that. I never get these names quite straight.

But you never turn around. How do you know? How *could* you? She all of a sudden feels spied upon in her delicate ministrations. If life is this vague, this mysterious, then someone must be following the novelist too. No, she decides, I am entering too much into the spirit of things. I am embellishing his game.

Unasked, he declares that he watches the storefront windows, and although the image is slewed by the big plate glass, he sees the novelist behind them both, treading lightly as if in the bull ring, with the ballpoint pen out in the open and the covers of the little notebook gleaming like coal. Could the name be Jorge Madeiras? Not José or Juan, and not Menén—

Then, she asks, faintly irritated, does he see you watching him, and change his ways accordingly? Rather than a Spanish novelist, he may well be a detective from Montmartre who just happens to have mistaken you for someone else. Not all people who look like writers *are*.

No, he just *knows* what the man is, but not who.

Then, she says loudly, if I ever see him I'll ask him. We can't have people of that caliber following us about without knowing who they are. And why.

I could be famous, he says with a wince. I am. That's how those people work. They sneak around and watch. Then they go home and turn you into a lasting presence.

At first she scoffs, then relents. Why should not a Rat Man have a Boswell in the streets? Never mind how imaginary. If she were Rat Man, and she is not wholly sure she is not, then she too would want a follower. All he's doing is to arrange himself into myth. Another little quirk, more easily indulged than denied, it falls at once into the basket of his personality. In its minimal way his life has put out a new bloom. No, a precious petal of illusion. Yet it is by illusion that he lives, survives. She vows to look behind her when she walks behind him, but more willing to find the statue of Balzac trundling along behind her than a flamelike Spaniard with a little book. José-Juan-Jorge Madero-Madeiras-Menéndez. Oh, she yearns, for a simple name like Camus or Gide. Do French writers live in Spain? Then why should Spanish—no, Sharli, she corrects herself: Franco drove them out. Still, Franco's long gone. We've other demons among us nowadays. Could José Et Cetera have come to Paris for *him?* Not Rat Man, not Poulsifer, but—

I'll check, she says. Maybe you have a friend. In a neat little blazer with yachting buttons? Brass against navy blue?

No, he says. In a short-sleeved woollike shirt with a roundish collar. I have seen him. A very haunted-looking man, quite young, and his face is familiar. Juan Somebody.

From the newspapers? Now she understands.

No, says Rat Man, completing his fabrication, I have seen him at the tables, heard him being addressed in Spanish, or maybe Portuguese, and signing copies of his books. They sit and drink and wait for people to identify them. It is the aggressive form of humility.

She is not going to quarrel with that. Once again he is making sentences, hauling up into view something more than a boy's vocabulary. There is hope. If self-deception gets him going, then let it. Anything that gives him back a piece of his lost life makes her rejoice. Now, as rarely, she glimpses the life she could still have were there no Rat Man to tend, and she wonders who appointed her to this, and how long it will go on. She has a career, of course, but apart from that a private life both marginal and plain. I was always looking for a burden, she tells herself; I found one. I was ideal for him. I have very few needs myself. And now, even as I tend him to the best of my ability, he goes wandering off into a wonderland of his own, with imaginary courtiers and retainers. A Boswell yet. Who never speaks. Who is never there. Who, if he exists at all, is some lecher coming after *me.* I'm not that bad. I have thighs. A slight swilling sway in my high-heeled walk. I am voluptuous. I have been with eighteen men in my life, but I have not been with Rat Man eighteen times. A few times a year he can be brought to it, but it ends as fast as snow in Nice.

Unfair, she berates herself. I chose to do it, I am doing it, I shall go on doing it, whatever the motive. I prefer honor to happiness. No, I have actively chosen honor. Well, if not honor, then service, in the tradition of all the self-denying spinsters: self-esteem and self-abuse. I belong among the dutiful daughters who, if they are lucky, become teachers and nurses, librarians and senior secretaries. If they are luckier still, they creep away once a year, to Arles or Budapest, to see what life might have in store for them. A life folded over and sealed up like an envelope. She draws back from completing her list of dull fruitions. Rat Man will more than do, she decides. How long can he last like this? In real terms, he was done for as a boy; he has lasted this long only through an almost holy obliviousness. He endures by setting himself at naught. By pretending his face is made of rotten sackcloth, his body of lath and plaster held together with big looping rubber bands. It is quite a technique. If you insist you are nothing, you will always be something. If you are worth nothing, then you do not ask for anything, but you always end up with something.

Without warning, he plants a kiss, a dry one, on the bridge of her nose, nuzzles for a while, then tells her he can see she is having second thoughts about him. At least the Beast in the movie had a chance of becoming a handsome prince, whereas a Rat Man will only ever become more horrible; his age will see to that. He does not believe in reincarnation, miracles, or medicine.

I'm getting old too, she says. I see a pension in the distance, and a room like yours, full of bills, with no telephone, no mail, no callers, just a lot of days to get through like walking up a circular ladder whose rungs do not know your name or even recognize the pressure of your feet. Freezing the thought, she hunts for old newspapers to give him. Give him entire? Why not? After all, the things she might not give him might be the very things to soothe him, while the uncensored cuttings might drive him into a twentieth-century frenzy. God, she caricatures him in an instant of blistering revenge, he will say: What's this? He will have discovered the wheel. Or this? He will have noticed electricity. Then she cheers up, having shed her pain, at least in the cell of her mind.

Whole newspapers she hands to him, new enough to grime his hands. Here, she says. Here is the world.

Where are we? She knew he was going to ask. They are inhaling the tonic air of late summer in her tiny patio, he on the ground on a poncho, she in the aluminum chair that blows about on windy days like a ground-bound kite. Will you clip now, or take them all with you? The scissors change hands. He stabs, he snips, he holds up the clipping to his face as if detecting warmth. Then he regales her with a world she already knows about, from how, according to the aborigines of Australia, koala bears embody the spirits of dead children, to the American President's remark that, if there is one thing about the United States that counts most of all, it is the fact that you can get rich there. She groans, he wonders at what.

Soon he goes his way, bundle of newspapers under his arm, his pockets stuffed with cookies, and a ham sandwich rammed inside his shirt. He knows it will not fall. But, instead of going home to the Street of the Cat Who Fishes, he does an ever-widening tour, deliciously postponing the moment of his next read. He feels as if he has lived a lifetime in this day, a Saturday of course. He arrives at a soccer game in progress although almost over, applauds the end of the game without troubling to find out the score, and remains at the ground long after even the groundsmen have gone.

First, though, they re-lime the penalty spot in front of both goals, and he walks out to watch them, nodding gravely at the care with which they work. He likes to see the game of rough-and-tumble, of lissom strides and nifty passes, but he prefers the field empty, no bodies interrupting the long taper of the white lines, the broad netting behind the goal mouth. He squats in the goal to read in the mellow sunlight, as unobserved as unobserving, and, in a wholly unselfconscious series of impromptu motions, fashions a paper hat from sheets discarded, a paper glider that is too floppy to fly well, and a paper trumpet through which, hearing Louis Armstrong, he toots at the swallows as they soar and twirl, then at the worm-hunting starlings on the ground. Right on the center spot, from which a player taps the ball to start the game, he feels aligned with everything that counts. Then it rains, and he wards off the drops with more newspaper, fashioning a small white roof as if he were a sitting saint in a shrine.

Two scoffs at himself later, he has found a better shelter by far, and, first at the crouch, then lying full length, he disappears from view behind a sign saying *Bière,* which happens to be a shoulder-high canvas tent pegged to the ground just outside the touchline. This is better than what he has in the Street of the Cat Who Fishes. The rain taps above him, thwarted and mysterious, while he tries to read while lying down. Now the newspapers fall against his face, lagging him, making him safer than ever, and he does not hear the sparrows that flutter-strut into the shelter to join him. One of his longest sleeps ensues, in the course of which he rotates his body a full 360 degrees around its axis.

Eight

Soon after the Sunday soccer game begins, he wakes. It is midmorning and he wonders if he is close to the airfield. No sound of planes, though. When he crawls out, the game halts briefly as he draws attention. Somewhat scared, he kneels and goes back in, but they urge him out, shoo him past the touch-line with his bundle of newspapers, which he has half rolled up to make a weapon. More like a muff, though it is no use to him, it makes an excellent cushion on which to sit and watch the game. At halftime he wanders away as if summoned by the referee's whistle. The players stop, but he begins, not running, but leaving the ground with a rolling motion of one who rides the surface of the earth with wary delight. It stays beneath him, at the same speed as he walks, but one step later it might not be there, and then he would have gone right through to be among the koala bears.

He goes home to read. He reads, he persuades himself, for France, just as someone else might play soccer or ride a bicycle. To begin with, he scans the front pages only, astounded that so much of the world has left him in the lurch. Not a sign of his presence can he find. Well, he is not news. Nor Sharli. Nor the little Spaniard who dogs his steps. Hundreds of others are, among which, at first casually, he finds a face that draws him, a name that rings a bell, then sets a whole belfry clanging as he flushes hotter than ever before, with the distinct sense that something is squeezing his skull, then letting go, then squeezing even harder. His eyes run, his heart jumps like a baby rabbit. His fingers tap a swift rhythm against his palm. He does not know what he is doing. He lights a match to set the page aflame, but abruptly halts, blows out the flame, and finds his magnifying glass. With shuddering hands, he aims the glass at the face. Far away, then near. Far away the face is upside down. Close, it is the right way up. Halfway, it tumbles and flows as the image hovers in optical no-man's-land, which he thinks is where he would like it to remain. Look, he tells himself. Make sure. The name is the key to the face. No, the face is key to the name. Did he ever see the face? He is not sure, but the name on the page collides with the one in his memory. One of the few intact faces he carries in his mind, not as one of the dead, but as one of the unthinkable, a human who should never have come into being in the first place.

What sort of face? A cardsharp's. A racecourse tout's. A vendor of filthy postcards, even. Small, sharp features, an air of affable deviousness, from the front at least, whereas the profile has the sag of cruelty. All droops. Not an ugly face, but that of a third-rate movie actor or man-about-town down on his luck. Bad temper roams about in it looking for a place to settle. It is, he tells himself, a face that can look at just about any awful thing and still come away with more than a bit of good cheer left. Natty little fedora hat, the sort that is usually green, with a frisky multicolored feather tucked into the hatband; the back of the brim raked up, the front tugged down toward the nose, the dangling cigarette, the two slight bags under the pointed chin. Polo-neck thin sweater, he notes, worn with a sports coat. Photograph taken in Peru, attributed to Gamma-Liaison/Nicole Bonnet. Both of them, in fact: the profile against no background save the white Arctic of newsprint, and the chatty posed one at the café table while the man in question fondles his newspaper with one hand. The small pot of coffee awaits his pleasure. The ashtray looks full. The sunglasses are in his top pocket, to guard his eyes from more than the sun of Peru or Bolivia.

This is *he,* the burner of churches, the baker of people. Rat Man falters. Can he be sure? Is this the man who gave the order, or just another of that man's kind? In a sudden mental swirl, he decides it does not matter. He goes to his records, pieces of newsprint and scrawled-on bits of frayed writing paper, all rolled in oilskin and locked in the wardrobe of the vacant doll's house. Never mind the name. This worldly, almost raffish-looking man, who meted out life and death from a polished desk not far from Rat Man's home village, has come all the way home, deported by a slow-coach regime.

Rat Man is amazed how much he knows; not how much he remembers, but how much he has acquired through simple porousness over the intervening years, when the entire affair was in cold storage. Year by year, some years more than others, it has reached him and sunk in, via the clippings that have come his way. He gasps to think how many clippings he has missed, but he knows the outline of things, the major names, the ranks and the faces and the exact degree of guilt. Most of them, he knows, are dead, but here is a live one to do duty for all the rest. Rat Man just knows that, as well as being double-manacled by arms and legs to two rings in the cement, the survivor from Peru stands in deep water with a mouth full of thumbtacks, his mouth taped shut, and only rabid rats for company. Oh, the authorities will keep him well, make no mistake, until, until, the day. Rat Man smiles explosively, and then he tries.

He tries to say the name. It will not come. He tries to say the rank. *Haupt—* He gets that far. What language can this be? *Haupt-sturm—* He halts, wringing wet. Then says the end of it, the most hateful word of all: *führer.* What it adds up to is captain: not much of a rank with which to wipe out six hundred and forty-two villagers. He sometimes thinks he makes six hundred and forty-three, then thinks of the number as 643. It is over sooner. He peels open clippings from 1953 that tell how twenty-one Nazis were tried for the atrocity, not one of them an officer, but fourteen of them conscripted Alsatians, from his native region. He heaves drily. Bits of facts soar from the newsprint toward him, telling him nothing. The names are not the names of soldiers or even people.

He reads haphazardly, with loathing, wondering what all this has to do with him; if nothing, then why is he so upset?

Nobbe, a German, pleads guilty, but is adjudged insane and goes his way to a mental home. Pfeffer, another, says yes he killed people, he shot at their chests, he was ordered to do it on pain of death. Lenz, a warrant officer, says he took no part in any massacre, but spent the time strolling around the village, trying to appreciate it. Lies, says Boos, a sergeant; Lenz had thrown hand grenades among the women and children in the church.

Look, Rat Man, the liars are weaving tales again. Here comes a man who wants to enter the village to pick up his tobacco ration. They turn him back. Here comes a music professor who insists on speaking to one of the officers already within the sealed-off village. They let him through. He sees Boos shooting. A woman in the blazing church screams to Kahn, a captain, that she is not French, but he shoves her back into the fire. Yes, Busch admits, I shot people at the garage. Graff carries brushwood into the church, dumps it on the bodies. Daab denies it all. So does Ochs, who told Steger to leave an elderly woman alone, but Steger shot her anyway, and Ochs took ricochets in the legs. Grienberger fired high, he says. Löhner, white-haired with the quiet manner of a pharmacist, says he is truly sorry he had to carry brushwood into the church. Yes, he says, Boos did shoot and throw grenades, and he saw Kahn hand out bottles of liquor. Boos denies having baked the eight-week-old baby. Höchlinger, an Alsatian, says he slept under a hedge during the entire operation.

The presiding judge, with the musical name of Saint-Saëns, expresses his amazement that, with so many Nazis taking a nap, behaving like tourists, helpfully steering people away from the danger zone, and at worst aiming to miss, anyone died at all. He has to go on conducting the wake. Only three out of twenty-one express regret. Lenz gets the death sentence, like his accuser Boos. The others receive sentences of from ten to twelve years, mostly at hard labor. Forty-two absent Germans they condemn to death in absentia. Only two years later, the death sentences on Lenz and Boos become hard labor; all the sentenced Alsatians save Boos have slipped back into Alsace, and five of the seven Germans have gone home because, awaiting trial, they have already served more years than their sentences demand.

The mayor rips the Croix de Guerre from the town hall in the new, barracks-type village; the president of the Families of Martyrs Association removes the Légion d'Honneur from the graveyard. And Rat Man, dazed in a glaze, hears only inconsequentially lethal names exchanging long-forgotten roles: what Ochs says Daab claims Kahn saw Boos doing with Lenz helping. It is dead straw. It will not catch, it will not feed. It has already soaked up blood. The over-and-done-with he has to leave alone, but his mind lurches toward what the clippings tell him about those who never came to trial at all. Was it these who, while taking a nap during a nature walk, aimed high to miss and guided people away from the danger zone only to stuff them into the burning church or the heated oven? With an awful heat beneath his chin, he deciphers names at the squat, there in his drab little kennel:

Brodowski. General. Shot in 1944. Account closed.

Lammerding. General. Lung cancer, 1971. Helped by the British. Too many cigars during retirement.

Kleist. Sergeant major. Of the Gestapo. Fate as yet unknown. No, a minor pigeon, compared with

Dickmann. Major. Killed in 1944. And

Kahn. Major. Bigger game, Rat Man. Wounded, lost an eye. Last heard of in Sweden, 1953. The animals depart, he whispers, they all have places to go to, but there are never enough of them in graves. All I need is a trousers press, a good hot iron, some needles and thread or fine wire, and I will have me a merry little afternoon, fusing them together, blending them, sewing up their mouths. He has saved the sheep's eye for last, but he still has not said the name or formed it to his mind's ear. If this is not the man, it is that man's superior. Good enough. He tries again to utter the name, to see it behind his closed eyes like someone receiving telepathy, but all that comes is the dapper, thick-lipped face. Anyway, he calms himself, if this is not the man, then it is that man's superior's immediate subordinate. Or that man's subordinate's immediate superior. Making, in each case, the same man. Oh, we have him all right, his name is— He coughs, chokes, expectorates, almost hurls his quaking body after what he has spat up, a coke, a cinder, a hunk of broken floorboard, and murmurs Poulsifer to the floor.

Wrong again, that is his own hardly ever used surname, squashed by Americans into Pussyfoot.

Once more he does his best, squeezing the man's face until his name leaps from it to befoul the air of the Street of the Cat Who Fishes.

Nothing, still. He calls up the dumb, the blind, the maimed, to help him say the word. Any of those other, wooden-sounding names will do. He mouths them: Nobbe, Lenz, Pfeffer, Boos, Kahn, Busch, Ochs, murmuring why do

I remember *them,* and then he goes afield, saying almost anything that sounds barbaric enough, from *schnell* to *los* (his German comes from movies, Alsatian-born as he is), from *achtung* to *heil. Beethoven,* he says. It breaks the spell, breaks the babble. His mouth forms to receive the word from his mind, his throat; yes, to expel it from his system, into the aforementioned air of his tiny street. But only air comes. He is alive. The air proves that. Is he a leaf exhaling? It could be poison. Then he is no leaf. Only humans exhale poison. Leaves are good. He recognizes that, while the criminals have gone free, he has just put in a life sentence of his own for what was done to him and his. His rage boils up again. He wads the clippings to hurl them or grind them underfoot, except his feet are bare, then sets them gently down. *Boche,* he sighs, I'll call him *Boche;* just so long as Madame Guillotine snags the right neck. What's in a name? That name's whole history. I am not Rat Man, by preference, for nothing. *L'homme des rats.* The man of the rats. *L'homme aux rats.* The man with rats. *L'homme rat.* The man rat. *Boche,* he says to himself with heavy, jagged emphasis, last heard of in Germany in the early 1950s. He's had a good run, and now we can go stroke him with long feathers on the exposed nerves.

Once outside, clippings in hand, he addresses the nearest policeman, loses his temper, and within the hour finds himself locked up—for what? He has no pants on. Sharli arrives right on top of a hard day's preparation for Monday's classes, and unspeakingly shakes her head. Rat Man has disgraced himself, she says.

No, he answers, Rat Man merely forgot himself; he went outside without going along with himself. He was still, mentally, indoors.

Quibbling, she tells him.

I was beside myself, he says. With rage.

That's what kills you, she tells him. You'd better take it steady. What's wrong with you anyway? You look as if you'd been dragged through a hedge backwards and slept out all night.

All true, he says. I slept at the soccer ground, under a tent that said *Bière.*

Beer? If you'd walk around with it on your back, they would pay you wages, have you considered that? She is angry with herself for not sifting his newspapers with ninety-nine percent thoroughness.

Obviously, she says, something has set you off. In the newspapers, I wouldn't doubt. What did I miss? After all. When all is said and done. I am not your keeper. Am I? *Am* I? Did you see yourself?

Not exactly, he whispers, but I saw my ghost. My father's, my mother's, my schoolmates'. I went to sleep with a head full of ghosts, and when I woke they, not the ghosts, were all playing soccer at the level of my head. I saw—the *Boche.* I call him *Boche.*

You would, she snaps. I know who. He surely doesn't need any help from you, old lad. Due process will take a year or two, then *pouf,* they'll parole him to write his memoirs in Lausanne.

I'll testify, he says gravely. I'm one of the few. I'll have a day in court, a month, a year. I'll never shut up. Off my chest for ever and ever. I'll offer.

To testify? Well, if you can stand it, you should.

I will, he says in a level tone. But I meant more than that. I will offer *my services.*

You never offer them to me. What services?

Well, if any interrogating needs doing. I've been thinking up a few ideas that ought to save them weeks of needless talking. Just give me a fisherman's needle. He'd remember things he never knew.

So that's it, she says, scolding and self-rebuked. No more rats. You'll be just like him.

Like him? Like me. I'll do a bit for each of the six hundred and forty-three. I'll practice, I'll start tonight.

Look, old lad, she says, they have experts, they don't need the likes of a bungling duffer like you, all banged up and bunged up, never knowing where your last meal came from or your next. They don't need amateur torturers, they've got pros, they've got scores of grown-up lads who used to disembowel cats. What do they need with an old rat man, whose rats are plastic or fox furs, and who sleeps nights at the soccer ground? *Their* interrogators, my old duck, have nice, well-behaved children, carefully watered beds of roses, and beautifully spoken lady wives with credit cards who fill them full of veal and cheese and scrape the blood from under their hubbies' fingernails. They're the ones. Torture's got respectable, ever since they strapped the damned Algerians to planks. It's not a blue-collar activity anymore. Honest. Rat Man, you're behind the times. Mind you, I don't mind this little flood of testosterone. It's an ill wind that blows no good somebody's way. Now she wonders where she first heard about testosterone, a fluid that explained so much.

He tells her that he still intends to offer his services, and she can see the idea frothing and looming in his head. Trial by rat. Ordeal by rats. A whole column in the newspaper:

> The last person to visit the condemned was the notorious, though beloved, notable of the boulevards, Etienne Poulsifer, better known as Rat Man to millions the world over. When asked by Rat Man if he had any last requests, the arch-criminal merely answered, "A chance to finish the job." At this, Rat Man—

He recoils, not from the violence of his imaginings, but from his inability to think up anything harsh enough to inflict on the butcher of old. Insane and useless combinations occur to him—sausages, needles, hordes of rats, rat poison, strangling wires, a winding sheet of poison ivy or manchineel leaves—but they will not do. They fail to translate indignation into revenge. What is bad enough? He settles, against his raging will, for the quietus as practiced in New Jersey, with syringe and three lethal fluids. Too kind, he says, but it would be a novelty at least.

He is that child again, running cross-country to escape the Huns, but the more he tries to picture himself doing so the more his legs lose their rhythm. He stubs a foot, he stubs both, almost falls. On he sprints, not daring to look behind him, but when the left leg goes smoothly the right fumbles. Again and again he tries to follow the motion, praying that it will even out into a blur, but if it isn't a pothole it's a rock, if not a locked knee then a seized-up ankle joint. Replaying that movie, of something he's never seen, he trembles at its stutter, its hesitations. No, not the movie, but the boy in it, for some reason not to be coerced by the mind's eye into a smooth action. Not that the Huns catch up with him, but he either marks time or runs ragged. Why, he wonders, can't I picture myself doing it right? Why, when I try it, do I get a cramp in my leg, the leg of today, that forces itself back into my past and almost costs me my life?

After a while, he no longer tries to run freely in his mind. The scene tugs at him, though, like a rebuke from the dead.

Nine

Now, between a contrite kiss and a shamefaced grin, he sets out to surpass himself. We'll do it with decorum, he tells her. With pomp.

Not we, she says. You on your own. This is one of the things that never needed to be done. Only men would think of it. Only a man. Only a you. Why do I bother? You're crazy. The world is waiting. Get a job. Be modern. This is nineteen eighty-something. The century will soon be over. The Martians or whoever will soon be here. All the little Spanish novelists will be in exile again, on the moon. Why not try, my old vagabond, to have one sensible idea before it all shuts down? You've no more chance of tinkering with that man's innards than you have of marrying Joan of Arc.

Trust me, he says. I've ways. I'll get *men.*

You've been through enough, my old sponge, my young crusader. You wouldn't want to have to relive that lot again. I'll be damned if you ever get another newspaper from me.

It's in the air, he says. It's endless. It's the only way to the end of time. To reach the end, you often have to go back to the beginning. Know how they worked it? Three stages: One. Surround the chosen village. My, that was quick. Two. Occupy the main offices, see. Police, post office, town hall. We're getting there. Three. Round up everybody in the square, not neglecting—in those days—using the town crier to spread the word. Nowadays they'd use TV. And it would say: Those who do not come outside immediately to be shot will be shot. It was like that in the olden days, when I was a kid.

Then, she insists as she steers him into his own street, for the love of Jesus crucified and the sanity of those who're left and looking after you, won't you be *said?* Leave it alone. Go back to ratting.

Just like in the town of Bulle, he says musingly. Not far away. That was another one. The hangmen were all volunteers. There's a funny delicacy in that. More for sport than anything. Ninety-nine from lampposts, trees, and balconies. Now, rats don't make that kind of sport out of other rats, despite their rotten reputation. Then they played the gramophone at the Tivoli Café and all got smashed. That was at Bulle, not far away. With things like that in the air, you'd wonder—if you were grown-up at the time—if the end of the world had begun; but, when it didn't, when it was as much as another day in coming, a whole other day, you wondered instead if the end of the world would ever begin, and then, once it was underway, if it would ever stop.

Home, she says. This is bad talk.

It was bad stuff.

I believe you, every word, she says. Don't make a meal of it, a banquet. Don't make a pig of yourself about it. She feels coarser with every word, and he, in turn, senses the futility of telling her why, essentially, he has been so occupied with it as to go out without his pants on. He has made the news again, snapped by a photographer. Or so he supposes. The trouble is, none of those who know of Rat Man know Rat Man's story. He would love to do it in mime right there in the street, with the fox fur cached inside his coat: "Leddiz an' gennermen, my name is a German name—Ochs-Boos-Daab—and I run around, just like this, bap-a-pap-pap with my machine gun. Plug the little Frogs. Get them all."

In his mind's eye he scuttles around (Sharli trying to shove him through the weird upward-opening door of his place), aiming to miss and killing everyone in sight, and then he shoves all the bodies and the rest of the living into the church. Big bundles of hay and brambles. In it goes. He lights the fire. He is everywhere, as Daab-Boos-Ochs, or Boos-Ochs-Daab, obeying orders as fast as he can. A Hun.

Now his mood changes. He worries that he won't live long enough to see the execution.

See it? Sharli is aghast. You mean: Be alive when it happens, if it does. You surely don't suppose they'd let the public—

Whichever, he says numbly. I'd like to be in the vicinity. Give a helping hand. A cheer. A little wish that it be very painful for him. It's called a grudge. You know, in Greenland they have no jails. They just lock you up for the night, then let you out. Even murderers. The weather's jail, see.

I don't spend much time there, she says, wanly abstracted, her mind not on the topic at hand but fixed on the world of waitresses: tables with puddles on them, tips left in the slop, hands red and cuticles peeling or frayed from all the fetching and carrying. She is glad, all of a sudden, she teaches school; she is creating the future.

Without a word, Rat Man moves away from her and, instead of going inside, walks back the way they have come and lifts up a chunk of rock from the street, carries it back to her with enigmatic tenderness and says: They make cement with milk these days.

The nothing she says is not enough. It's dangerous there, where it was, he says. She tells him to put it down among the other trash, and then the insects will have a Gibraltar. He doesn't, though, he muses for a moment, then walks all the way back and puts the lump exactly where it was, ready to cause an accident all over again.

Now she asks, and he just shrugs: I don't have the right, he says.

Then if you don't have the right to that, you don't have the right to much. You really don't. His astute and almost nimble face seems to bulge with grief. She withdraws what she said; it was too harsh. Once again he is lost in a pattern he dare not break. What amazes her is that he took the trouble to move the thing at all. Almost always he sides with gravity, feeling somehow safer in that. If, she wonders, his pants fell down, would he leave them be? It is possible; it would depend on the weather, perhaps, but just as possibly it might depend on nothing at all. Nothing would have any bearing on the situation, and his pants would stay down.

They go inside, arrange their bodies to fit the tiny space full of the aroma of decaying newspaper. She asks him to air it out. Open that so-called window. No, he says, the room will fill with soot. They hug. She has to leave. She is involved in the world, in its conscienceless onrush. She gets paid. Rat Man is involved in distant vibrations, entering a phase of hearty paralysis, with a new rage feeding him.

She goes. It feels to him, as she picks her way through the Street of the Cat Who Fishes, that he is backing away from her. But he has an idea, one that makes him smile. It went off like an alarm clock in his head. Out he goes, only a few minutes after Sharli. There at the xerox machine, with a few coins in his fist, he copies the newspaper face whose name he dare not speak. Then he asks. More coins. It blows up blacker than in the newspaper, but not more white. The face looks haggard now, subject to weird internal twists of the spirit, five times bigger than the original.

When he leans over a desk and shows it to the policeman on duty, a man far too young to know about the burning village church, he gets nowhere at all.

Out in the sunshine he aims his face at the sky and wonders if this might not be the best weather of all: dry, tonic, self-effacing. Then he goes home.

Soon he is in the street again. If, at the copy center, he was like Humpty Dumpty at a nuclear reactor, here is back among his tribe, streetwise, and with a new thing to do. He has attached the top of the blowup to a length of stick, and he can wave it like a matador's cape with sword concealed. He does, and in a reflex action passersby avoid him, swerving, stepping back, stopping short. Soon he reaches the tables, which are packed, and he envies them all the brisk buzz of mildly intoxicated conversation. Those familiar with him await the rat, the fox, whatever he has inside his coat. The heat under his chin is terrific, but he persists, rigging the xerox to face the sun and fishing the magnifying glass from his pocket. Soon the angle is right and the sun sends a scalding white dot he cannot look at. It browns, it smokes. The eye is catching fire. The sun burns it away, leaving only a hole whose edges glow briefly as he blows into it. Those watching laugh and egg him on. He needs no second bidding and continues, holding his breath as he kneels, and letting his tongue sag out like a child intent.

Ten minutes later, thanks to the sunny day, he has perforated the face with holes of varying sizes, almost as if it has been peppered with shots from guns of different bores. Something grievous in the ruined paper reminds him of a saint, but he knows better. He accepts the coins, the paper money, the applause, then shakes his head when they call him Rat Man and ask for a different show. No, he tells them, he is at the beginning of a new act. It will cost more. Those who operate the copy machines will get to know him. He wonders how big the biggest blowup would be.

The sky's the limit, someone tells him.

No, he answers at his profoundest. The sky's the thing you put the limit to.

He doesn't feel too bad. His life has come to life again. No, he can't say that. You can't say that. He has found something to do; and, although it isn't enough, it will do for the meantime. All over Paris he will carry the face and plug it with holes made by the sun. He will burn people's initials into the cheeks, the brow; he will brand swastikas on the chin. It is a way to go, requiring no rat. Now, how, he wonders, does the doll's house relate to this new occupation? He can roll up his supply of blowups and store them under the roof. He thanks the sun for giving him something new to do; he thanks glass, paper, and wood for a new destiny fraught with golden possibilities. Half dreaming right there in front of his fans as they get back to talking, since the show seems over, he links himself to the serious artists—the writers, the painters, the sculptors, the composers—who, all their lives, afraid that this year may be their last, race to get a piece of work finished, and then realize they have survived and will have to start all over again under the same benighted assumption. Years later, he thinks, they look back on not quite satisfactory books, paintings, sculptures, symphonies, they could have taken their time over. Or does that haste to finish energize them all the more? Had they not rushed things, they might not have survived; going slow, they would have dwindled to a halt and died, not known what they now know they wish they did not know.

He gasps, accepts the proffered glass of wine, which goes to his head right away. He goes home, sleeps, wakes, grins a complete grin at the surrounding vacancy, and sleeps again, in a trivial way fulfilled, but half knowing he cannot go on repeating himself for the next several years. When he wakes, he seems to have much smoother nerves. There are a thousand ways to go. Why, he wonders, was I worrying?

Over the next few days, and not without winning back some of the attention he used to claim with his rat, he experiments in the street. He makes a banner of the blowup, then burns the entire face away, starting with a big swastika. A few cheers build into a commotion of applause. They know whom he's burning. Then he tries wheeling the blowup about, affixed to the hood of an ancient English-style perambulator filched from a junk heap. It is harder for them to see this; the banner is better. He tries to combine the banner with a rat, or the fox fur. He ties the magnifying glass to the fox's snout, and actually arranges the fox until the face begins to char. But this is too cumbersome. More dangerously, he holds the blowup over his own face and aims the glass as best he can, braced for the little stab of heat as the rays burn through. This, potentially more morbid an exercise, wins him a bigger audience, who half suppose he intends to brand himself as well. The police warn him, but he shows them his unhurt face, protests his skill with the glass. No one really cares that much. The sun is common property. Now, if he were burning trash, he would be in trouble; but, because what he does is somehow a ritual, a charade, he gets away with it. The money comes in. He has not had so much money in years, but his expenses have increased, and there is no telling what Sharli will do when she finds out. She will not stop him, though. What does she say on such occasions?

We'll live, she says; only time dies. It comes from the movies, this maxim. Well, then, he is killing time, burning it, shooting holes right through it. A small boy could do it just as well, a sorcerer's apprentice, but a small boy is what in some ways he still is. The thought warms him. In a year or so, he will have a following; fans will escort him through the streets and he will perform in the most august cathedrals, clad in satin robes.

I don't care, Sharli says, after seeing him at work. It pays the rent. So long as you feel happy with it. If it's what you have to do. And doing it eases your mind, then that's ducky, my old burner at the stake. Just don't blind yourself playing with the sun. Who was that old Greek who did? Maybe not a Greek.

A Greenlander? He sees someone clad in furs, warming his nose with a glass aimed at the feeble sun, and getting no help at all, only a frozen nose. Thank you, God, he says aloud, for planting me in Paris.

Ten

All of a sudden, it is a Paris less threatening. There is rain, wind, rudeness, true, but the sweet-sour aroma of Gauloises seems to him the breath of heaven. The city has tuned in to him again. The involuntary thing he does has won them over. Good. He does not have to try so hard. Doing what comes naturally is perfect for him. He cleans up his hovel. Scrubs his comb under the outdoor tap, using the ancient toothbrush, even though this smears his comb when, before, it was only caked with fluff and dandruff. A pink thing, much bigger than combs men use, it comes from Sharli, a castoff. Amazing, he thinks, how much hair I still have left: omen of a long life lived without benefit of clergy, voting, or the dole. He considers a change of outfit, something stolen or bought from the military surplus store; maybe a tunic with epaulets, and some kind of high-fronted U.S. Army Air Corps cap with an eagle to frighten birds away. No, he decides that would be too much the kind of thing he is performing against. He will go and look, for something lyrically anonymous, navy blue. Should he copy the clothes of the little Spanish novelist who follows him around? Not that either, he thinks, and shelves the question. Summer still hangs on; he can go about his business lightly clad for now. Will the winter sun ruin his act? By then, he hopes, his act will have developed into something else, doable indoors. He realizes that, all along, he has had the theater in mind, but he has no idea how to begin, how to make contact, but make it he will.

Lights, applause, deep red plush: that will be his life in the near future, and he will scuttle away each night to his scruffy bolthole. The contrast wins him with its whiff of royal degradation, its mix of grand and low, its hint of true worth's not needing to posture to itself in private. If only they would guillotine the Boche onstage, on a plinth of rich absorbent cotton. There would be only one performance, of course, but the buildup could be tremendous. Was it not thus in the old days? When justice had to be seen done. Was there not an audience for that? Nothing festive, of course, but all the trimmings.

For one short, grandiose instant, he considers how to interest the ruling powers in some such thing. A letter? A personal interview, in the course of which he shows clippings of an old atrocity? A telephone call? He has never phoned anyone in his life, but perhaps he should start now, having saved himself up for one utterly persuasive request, something so right and obvious they should have thought of it themselves. Why, thank you, Monsieur Poulsifer, for restoring us to our senses!

For the next few days, the banner serves him well. The blowups char. The sun obliges. Then there is rain and, from force of habit, he wanders the streets until the paper sags and breaks. Easy, he says, and has the blowup sheathed in plastic, using instead of the sun an old butane lighter he now has enough money to refill. Like a welder, he aims the sprig of light and melts the plastic, holes the face, in one motion. Not as many come to watch him during the rainy weather, but he doesn't need that many. What he does thrives in his mind. Even the real audience is in part imaginary; he has more control over it that way. Perhaps no one notices, but he develops a new finesse with his glass or the lighter, aims things better, ports the banner with even firmer dignity from place to place, site to site. Those in the know have already learned his route, his approximate hours. With a wry twist of his mouth, he grins at the thought of having almost a regular living, not quite eight to five, but getting there, almost as if he has become a responsible citizen.

Meantime, the real Boche sits in his cell somewhere out of sight, little knowing about Rat Man's latest reincarnation. Or so Rat Man thinks. A renegade part of his mind plays with the fancy that, somehow, the Boche has already heard about what is going on in the streets. If his face was not familiar before, then now it is.

Rat Man has done his work well. He moves abroad at night with a bucket of paste, a brush, and scores of Boche posters which, without providing the name, remind Paris of a Nazi face. Had he a team of helpers, he would cover more ground, but he makes at least some impact. It is now possible for two people to run into each other both of whom have seen the blowup face.

It's he, it must be.

A police trick?

No, *mon vieux,* some lunatic roams the streets and plasters the face all over Paris at night. Wait a week and the face will change.

It does not, though. Rat Man has now arranged a bulk rate at the copying facility. So far he has not enlisted the aid of Sharli; indeed, he sees less of her than hitherto, having an extra mission to accomplish. One day soon, everyone who watches him perform will have seen the poster, and everyone who sees the poster will have seen him perform.

Surely, he thinks, they won't conclude this is the face of Rat Man. Identify me with him by all means, but do not turn me into him. He considers adding a legend of some kind: The Face That Rat Man Burns. Or: The Face of a War Criminal. Neither sounds right. He wonders if he should plaster his own face all over Paris.

Paris is too big. The right size of place is the destroyed village, more to his scale; but he is a Parisian now, not a villager. Had Paris been destroyed, he would have felt the same way about the village. That would have made a permanent villager of him. Huddled with Sharli at the runway threshold, he confides some of this with expansive hand gestures such as she has never seen him make before. His voice is just a trace excited, his face more than a trace flushed. Yes, she decides: a monomaniac newborn. He doesn't even watch the planes.

But he watches her, wondering why when she speaks she opens her mouth a fraction wider than necessary, why when she makes consonants her tongue comes more into the open than it should. She wet-mouths her words. I am so lucky, he tells himself. He likes to watch her talk. Don't you get tired of that banner and the glass? she asks. He does, but he now thinks of it as a duty, his and his alone. No one else has the patience. Or the natural flair. You need to have had those awful things happen to you too. Otherwise, the whole thing is no more than a profiteering sideshow instead of—he stops —a holy crusade. The red diagonal cross on his shield must be plain to all. Plain as the runway on the ground is to the pilots in the air. He accepts and peels open a pink-and-white mint. They suck dozens of these while raptly watching, ignoring the kerosene smell from the jet engines.

You're in love with death, she says abruptly.

Not death, he says. Getting even. Finding my way to that face. Burning holes into it with—

You're getting narrower. You have more chance of shaking hands with an angel than of getting to him. He is beyond us all. One of the technically dead. Absent in the sense that means he no longer ranks as a human being. He's only the track of where he once was. Now, my old robin, have done, and leave him be.

He has gone too far, has come to dote on this face burning and poster sticking. Whatever is begun has its natural climax, provided you don't give up too soon. In five years it will all be over. He shows her the bulbous septum, the shiftily querulous face, the two folds of flesh under the jaw. He looks quite ordinary, she says. They always do. It's a cliché. I've seen him before. Everyone has. Better to burn holes in him than plaster his face on walls and doors. Or are you practicing black magic? You'll need a hair from his head if so, and a clipping from his nails.

Rat Man has not thought of this. His heart seems to be free-floating in its private area, pumping at random; but he can see the next step now. Seeing him tune in to it, she wishes she had learned to stop her mouth with newspaper. All you have to do is be intense enough, he tells himself. It's no good just mumbling over the bits, you have to work up a deadly passion and let it flow. He can see it now. Easy. Cheap even. And foolproof. Bribe the barber? Will they have a manicurist in there? Of course not. But they cut his hair, and, on the last day of all, they shave the neck brutally clean. The only trouble just now, chewing the last of the mint and holding Sharli's hand, he cannot link what happened to his family back then to what he wants to do. The missing link is himself, who keeps on changing.

Next weekend, Sharli decides it is time to distract Rat Man from his craving for revenge and ferries him out of the city a considerable distance to a small hotel which has a tiny warm pool still open. He cannot swim, but he lolls there in hip-high water listening to the Sunday bells, having for all she knows a rural ecstasy with a beginning smile that comes to nothing. Rapt, he can hardly talk. He is fueling up for the next round. Then they sit on chaises to dry. The sun has uncanny heat for the time of year, and this cheers him no end. He can go right back to work on Monday like other folk. He feels respectable, tells her so, but she lures him indoors to bed, joking that she can get a rise out of him yet, and she does, after diligent hugging. To egg on the squirt, he tactlessly observes, but he goes through with it, at last realizing what a wonderful woman is going to waste in his presence. He blames the war, but she tells him that blaming the war is like cursing Napoleon for the price of roses.

Very well, he declares. Just let me get *him,* not Napoleon, out of the way, and I'll mend my ways. I'll eat nothing but eggs and Spanish fly. You'll chafe nonstop from all my unwelcome attentions. You'll hardly be able to walk. You'll soon be slipping bromine into my chocolate to keep me quiet. He tinkers with the useless thermostat, trying to create a climate. It doesn't work, switched off at the source, so he begins to look at his penis through the magnifying glass, ogling it and marveling as it seems to turn somersaults, to flow and bloat, when he wiggles the lens about. With a mock-modest pout of the lower lip, he puts both organ and glass away.

In a pinch, not bad, he declares. It'll do. I have seen worse. Put to the test, he'd make a maiden squeak. If farmers only knew— He sees her studying him, her head shaking in disappointment.

Try *me,* she says with temperate bitterness. All I am is an impresario, a skivvy to fetch and carry for you. Lord knows why I took you on, but you'd better get famous soon, my puffin, or I'll have to trade you in for something more useful. Trade you in for a bicycle. Here. This is mouthwash. Use it. Don't swallow it. I could trot a mouse across your breath.

He does, using capful after capful, turning his mouth into a peppermint wasteland in which nothing can live. He feels as if he has rinsed out his mouth with scalding-hot soup, but once more his mind is on the target. She gives him a big sponge to play with in the bath, strews his bulk with a fluid that turns the water blue, the same blue as the pool, but he wanders off, all of a sudden resenting the palmy days the Boche must have enjoyed in Bolivia, Peru, Argentina, anywhere south of the border, sunbathing and basking, swigging the best wine and taking his croissants and coffee in the morning sun with a neatly folded newspaper by him. Yes, and going to the movies, choosing his books in stores, learning the language, dancing the rumba, the samba, the conga, the java, ogling the silky girls and pinching their behinds. All that jollity. Clean sheets and a four-poster bed with a little quiet garden outside full of tropical flowers in which, quiet as quiet can be, to mull over the atrocity, if he remembered it at all, no doubt long ago having supposed it was all done by someone else, with a quite different stroke of the pen.

Sharli is talking to him, but he is far away. Sometime soon, she says, we'll have to have those moles of yours attended to. Keep them out of the sun. Watch to see if they turn black. Then the foot doctor. She hands him the pumice stone to buff his heels with. Dry or wet, she says, you do it every day and keep the calluses thin. Especially as you seem to do more walking than ever now. We can't have you going onstage looking like that.

Rubbing away halfheartedly, he answers that they wouldn't be looking at his feet in any case. Well, she counters, if you were knocked down in traffic, you would want to have clean underwear, wouldn't you? Haven't you heard that one? By the same token, you'd want to have nice smooth heels. You never know who might look at heels.

Rat Men, he says with mock dignity, can go ragged. It goes with the trade. I was thinking about South America and how long he had there to have his fun and set up house. Sleep in late not just Sundays but all days of the week. Plant a little garden. Have his friends to dinner. Play cards. Bet on a few horses. Sample the best soccer in the world. All that. Imagine: he wipes most of us out and then buys a one-way ticket to paradise. And, when we finally catch up with him, we have to make do with all that's left of him. Trembling, I bet. With his liver wonky. His eyes getting fuzzy. His hearing mostly gone. His hair thinned out or blown away. We don't even get him back in what you might call buyable condition. It will be like polishing off a ghost. Like sinking a wreck.

Then leave him alone, she says, leave him to the authorities, who won't take things as personally as you. That's why they're there. They have the distance. He isn't worth your remaining days. Maybe they'll put him naked in a cage in the Jardin des Plantes.

Among the plants? I'm a zoo man myself. Kangaroos and lions. Even a certain kind of harvest mouse—

The zoo, then. Or the top of the Eiffel Tower in a special glass room. She tries to enter into the spirit of things, but the code of vengeance eludes her. She is dedicated to his life, not to his obsession.

Yet sometimes even he leaves his obsession behind. Before they check out of the hotel, he begins to collect up all the giveaways: the velvety shoe cloth, the samples of shampoo, the tiny wallet of threads and two needles. In case of later need. A well-traveled man, he decides, ends up with dozens of such things, to show off with, or just to arrange neatly on the bed, souvenirs of foreign parts. The Boche must have had hundreds of them from all his comings and goings across the frontiers. Maybe he has them with him in jail right now. And he is as he always was, down Bolivia way. Shoes like mirrors. Hair squeaky clean. Not a button dangling. He never went out unkempt.

Well, Rat Man tells Sharli, who is urging him to get a move on before they get charged for an extra half-day: A man that pure carries a snowball on either hand. If I was that pure, I'd expect to be nailed to a cross, and I'd provide the means as well. I'd hammer myself into place. It would be exactly what I'd been working towards.

Eleven

Back in Paris, without so much as a pause at the end of the airport runway to hold hands beneath as Sunday planes waft in on final approach, she notices how easily he tans. He has been in the sun only a couple of hours, but he has gone dark brown already, whereas she has a fair complexion she lards with number sixteen sunblock.

Even God couldn't find you under all that, he likes to say.

It isn't God, she usually retorts, who happens to be looking for me. Nobody's looking for me at all. I'm looking for myself most of the time, wondering what I did with my best years. I handed them over wrapped in fancy paper to a man who haunts the streets, who has floated through life like a moth working its way from one meal to another in somebody's knitting. I used to think that, when I finally took you in for something else, swapping you, you see, I'd get a sewing machine or a bicycle. I'll be lucky if I get a water pistol or a pair of bookends. You frittered yourself away on what can't be changed. You can, but *it* can't. Ever. And it will soon be too late to change you too.

Then something seems to come unstuck in her. One word drags another into the open, and she begins saying things for the sound of saying them, mounting from grumble to jagged tirade: No, nobody's looking for me. There never is. There was never a me. I was the stuff that waited in the cracks in the woodwork. What birds left behind in the nest when they flew away. That's me. Like the packing in a parcel. You spill it, rummaging for what's hidden underneath it, and it scatters all over the floor, the shape of chopped green beans, not sliced, if you know what I mean? Do you have the faintest idea what a chopped green bean looks like? On the scale of animal or vegetable beauty? Do you ever look at things as if they ever mattered to anyone? That's how your precious Nazis looked at folk before shooting them. Past them. Through them. Over them. I'd like an opinion poll, from God, Satan, Napoleon, De Gaulle, anyone you want, and what I want to know is this: Have you ever, any of you, Rat Men included, spent so much as half a second thinking about nothing but *me?* Am I considered at all, you precious prick of a man? Am I worth the time of day or never?

Rat Man says not a word, cannot even marshal his few thoughts as the crescendo builds then subsides, and she says to him, quite unaware of herself: Well, I think that's enough. You'd better calm down and pull yourself together.

As if he, Poulsifer, had said all this; he half believes he did, and lowers his head. She looks at him for quite a while in tolerant dismay.

So much of him seems not merely amateurish but primitive as well. Any time a bath is available, he does his laundry in his own fashion by climbing in full clad and soaping everything in sight. Then he peels off his socks, his underwear, his shirt and pants, and squeezes them all through until he lies there in a mounting scum the gray of elephant hide. His idea of cooking is to toss everything into one big pan and boil it to death. In the old days, when even to him his bedsheets were too greasy to be endured, he rolled them up and threw them outside, either for the police to arrest and launder, or until some kind soul gave him some more. As Sharli did. A combination of Robinson Crusoe, Harpo Marx, and Trappist monk, he prefers to eat off a folded newspaper, but she has initiated him to plates, though he prefers the paper variety, which he then rinses off outside if she doesn't catch him first. She cares because she is going to civilize him in spite of everything, even if it takes a lifetime. He is quite handsome when you clean him up, she says to herself, and he has great nobility of character. He has suffered, and we owe him something. He is my biggest child. What a shame he lives only, or mainly, in the world of play. He would not really mind if one day, assuming he could breathe underwater, we put him in a big glass room like one of those freshwater dolphins from the Amazon, and left him there to squint at folk who came to look at him, lolling his big flab and looking one hundred percent forlorn. Then they could put his pet Nazi by him in the next tank, and they could glare at each other all day through the glass. No, Sharli, she cautions herself, you are getting too logical. His destiny, if he has one at all and his destiny isn't already over, will be to waste himself in a thousand dismal little pointless enterprises until he drops. You'd no more ask a performing dog to recite the Sermon on the Mount. It's funny. It's as if the whole of civilization has to work within *his* limits until he decides that time is up. Then we can all please ourselves again. If I cut him loose for only a month, he'd be a walking wild man caked with filth and giving interviews to roaches. No, I'll see him through. I'll spruce him up while he thinks I'm really behind him in his—what is it? A manhunt, that's what it is. He's after big game.

After a neat little cry, she rounds up the used tissues and

wads them into an oblate ball, which she drops into the trash after first squeezing it tight to see how much moisture comes out. It only damps her hand a little. It falls among the tea leaves she refuses to pour down the sink. Nothing resists, she thinks. You can drop just about anything on anything and it won't mind. One day soon, everything will have turned into one big unresisting sludge and nobody will ever know we were here, fussing and arguing about who killed whom. With a sigh that comes down her nose, she pats the hair above her ears and arranges her notes for next week's classes. Her world is regular, clean, and loyal.

Whereas Rat Man's is almost total improvisation. He thinks the Boche is jailed in Paris. He wants the barber and has already established which bistro the prison staff wander into after hours. Not only is there a barber (he visits other jails as well) but there is also a whole team of warders (not so easy to convince) and of janitors (who, a different, less self-important order of beings, seem more approachable). In no time at all, after three cognacs, the equivalent of half a week's Rat Man wages, an Alphonse from Alsace has agreed to scoop up what he can from the two-room cell and bring it out in an envelope.

Nothing else mixed in with it, Rat Man tells him. It has to be pure. I mean, whatever it is, only from him.

Alphonse laughs. It's just like getting him out a bit at a time. If I bring enough, one day he'll be gone. All of him escaped. How about a bit of tissue?

Rat Man stares at him. Living tissue? That would be going too far too soon. All the same, the idea plucks at him and he envisions the scalpel, the scrape, the flake of skin held aloft for the light to catch, then the refrigerated cylinder that keeps it live. Or fresh. Uncontaminated at least. He is vague about the exact status of recently attached tissue.

Nothing like that, says Alphonse. What he might have wiped his mouth or nose on, see. *Papier pelure.*

How about a hair off his comb? Rat Man can already feel

his victim escaping by being blurred with someone else. No bit of anyone, he decides, is immediately recognizable once severed from the rest. A head, yes, or a scarred hand, some teeth like no one else's. A leg would be harder. A toe. Not to mention the heart, the pancreas, the bladder. Of those you could never be sure.

I'll try for a hair, Alphonse tells him. Who knows what might come with it as a bonus? We all lose some every day to the brush, the comb. I'll try, I really will. It's not much to ask, really. It's the first time I've had any call for prison souvenirs. It may take a few weeks, but we can meet regularly for a touch of cognac and I'll report whatever progress has been made.

Within a week or not at all, Rat Man says severely. If not then, I'll try someone else. He is amazed at how easy it sounds. He asks and he just about receives. No one has ever asked before. It takes originality to come up with something like this. Yet he has heard about boxes of Adolf Hitler's nail clippings going for a price, and isn't Napoleon's penis viewable in some museum? The problem is going to be what he does with the hair when he gets it. How convert it into a deadly weapon? Must there be drums, a still-warm rooster whose throat is cut, an obeah woman, a big fire and hundreds of chanting believers? He postpones the exact technique until Alphonse delivers. Maybe black magic can be watered down.

First comes a hand-sized piece of tissue. Rat Man looks at it with disdain. Then Alphonse produces a bit of cardboard with a hair attached by means of insulation tape. Alphonse is not very clever. A redhead, he plucks his own at a cognac a hair. They shout. Alphonse blusters, then confesses. He buys Rat Man a double cognac, which Rat Man sips and leaves. Alphonse promises to mend his ways. At length he produces the real thing. It looks different, at any rate. Who knows? Would the Boche recognize his own? Rat Man has so far referred to him only as the Nazi prisoner from Peru. How many can there be in one jail fitting such a description? Now

Rat Man is broke and has to work the boulevards nonstop in order to pay for blowups. It is important to keep the face before the public eye.

Now he sees the grim side of this escapade. There is too much trust involved. Who knows what bargains the prisoner himself has not struck in the jail? When Sharli reminds him, after a hard week's teaching, that she saw on TV a report, although without actual footage of the event, of the Boche's transfer ten days ago to the St. Joseph jail in Lyon, Rat Man squats in his hovel and allows the tears to flow. For himself, for Alphonse the corrupt, for Sharli, whom he keeps on deserting to follow his prey. An hour later, though, he is asking about trains, putting the question to his fans, and setting about earning the train fare. He informs them all he is going to move his show to the town in question. To be nearer the source. To offer his services to the public prosecutor. To breathe new air. Far from asking Sharli to ferry him there over a weekend, he resolves to make a point of being independent. Somehow, he just knows it, he will get there and, once there, strike home like a cobra. Lumbering across the fields, thumbing his way along the roads, clambering over gates and hedgerows, he will arrive, heaving forward like a plague of the old-fashioned furies with his butcher's knife, his three hypodermics from New Jersey, his map of the city, and, most important of all, the illicit map of the prison and its hollow walls. Before it even happens, across the furrows and pastures he tromps, complete with rucksack, heavy Irish walking stick, and a hundred blowups carefully rolled into a cardboard mailing tube. In a word: equipped. In another: ready. For the fray. Time, which up to now has merely elapsed, has begun to assume a shape aimed at a point in space. He bursts into snatches of uncouth song. Thinking of the fatuous Alphonse, he bursts into erratic laughter, startling his fans, who have never even seen him smile; a sweetened sneer was all he gave them. When he finds a flower, he wears it, determined to be dapper in his bungling way.

You'll soon be off, then, she says. Where will you live?

I could get myself arrested, he says. And jailed. Then I could work from the inside. No, I suppose I'd be far away from the likes of him. Better from outside. I'd have more freedom of action.

She stares. To do what? She asks him again. What did you have in mind? Just reaching him? Just having a chat? Filling his cell with rats? Giving him a good talking to? Sulfuric acid in his good-night drink? I can't imagine what. Besides, I have my cold.

Lemons, he says automatically, and garlic. *They're* the remedies. Already his dream has become ornate. On a horse speckled like a Dalmatian, he leaps across a chasm while plucking at his turban. Others have preceded him, on brown or gray chargers, riding sidesaddle or actually turned backwards, while those who seem to be prisoners await their arrival, each one immobilized in a man-deep bed of rocks. Only their heads are visible. Like that, he says. They're hard to get at, but they can't go away. She asks about the *they,* but he waves away her query, reminding her about lemons and garlic. How puffy she looks. Her normally out-fluffed hair has matted into pseudo-ringlets. She has a fever too. It grieves him that she can feel as hot as he, but clearly she is suffering, and he offers to swab her down. Cold water from the outside tap, he says, that will cool your face and forehead. She shakes her head, no longer surprised that someone so far out of the world of ordinary custom should entertain the idea of dispatching someone from it. There is nothing he would hate to leave, she thinks bitterly, if only he could stop that other life.

Even a rat has life, she murmurs. A right to it. Then she remembers: if he weeps, a lump or two of sugar will soothe him. They sometimes play doctor and listen to each other's heart, ear hard against the ribs. Most people's faces age over a lifetime, but his gains or loses years in seconds. All of his life is on top of him all the time.

I've grown backward, he whispers, tapping right palm

against left knuckles. I have grown forward, onward, in time, but my heart is backward. My heart is on backward, as we say of shoes.

Then, she says thickly through her congestion, make it behave. Make it give you a chance. Me too.

Too late. It jumps about. It would like to get into the open air, away from me.

I'll catch it if it does, she tells him with a faint attempt at levity. I'll never let it get away. I'll have a hand.

Shaking his head, he sees a crossroads ahead of him. He has to choose between Sharli and the prisoner from Peru. Or could he perhaps have both? Would he give up the prisoner for her? History has aligned him, he feels, whereas she has kept him on the rails until now for this precise purpose. All he is is an instrument, a weapon. Much of his life is empty in the way an eggcup is empty, but its concavity implies eggness, even though it might accommodate paper clips, rubber bands, or useless foreign coins. The eggness lingers. So, when he tries to take stock of his limited world—Sharli, the youth at the copy center, his fans, the soccer players, the various policemen with whom he has argued, not to mention Alphonse and the little expatriate Spanish novelist who dogs his steps—he knows his life cannot accommodate much more. It is all he can manage. Lord God, he murmurs: what richness, what abundance, I lead a crowded life, never mind what they say. Then there are all the voices of the ones I hear but do not even know. Plus this phantom from South America, the demon who came home to roost after plowing through my childhood. It is almost too much, keeping it all in balance. I would be better dead than worn away like this. If only someone would take it off my hands. I can't even keep it straight. What happened, Rat Man? Now he really tries. He does know, but vengeance has blinded him. Sometimes, like a mad dog, he tells himself, I can't see for foam and froth. Now what really happened to that Boche? Let me get it straight. Get it through your head, once and for all, she tells me. She knows. She reads with care whereas I, I read with—I get excited.

First they jailed him in La Paz. A whip-round among his Nazi friends took care of that. Oh to have Nazi friends. He went free, but only into jails a long way away. They did not even extradite him, they dumped him out like garbage. An army Hercules took off and, three hours later, he was in French Guiana, not that bad a place to be, from which a DC-8 flew him to Orange. He was never in Paris at all. First he was in the Montluc Fort, Orange, and then they took him to where he is now: the St. Joseph jail in Lyon. Couldn't he have been in Paris just a day? An afternoon, then? What's it matter? If you're famous you're everywhere all at once.

He goes on dreaming up the hated image, glad to have pinned him down, free of all Alphonses.

Not such a big man after all. Married with a daughter. And a son. Expert in Jewish affairs. Iron Cross, second class, 1941-ish. Only ever captain. *Chef du commando extérieur de la Sipo-Sd de Gex* near the Swiss frontier. He was the man who said his aides weren't tough enough. 1943, Iron Cross, first class. With sword. Pat on the back from Heinrich Himmler.

Installed at the Hotel Terminus (ironic name for many), near the Perrache station, Lyon, he amassed a notable score: 14,311 arrested; 4,342 assassinated; 7,591 deported. Plus, Rat Man notes, tumultuously, six hundred and forty-three others. Twenty-six thousand, he says, eight hundred and eighty-seven.

Always carried a bullwhip.

Competent amateur pianist. Moonlight sonatist.

Made shadow rabbits for children on the wall. Long thumbs: big ears. Mister Quicksands.

Abstemious too. Well, Rat Man is going to narrow the Boche's diet even further, in either Lyon or Orange or Paris, it almost does not matter where. He will pose as a newspaperman, gain access by becoming a jailer, a janitor. He will be an Alphonse, or even, out of the blue, become a superlative barber, cutting the hair of the top politicians as well as that of the prisoner from—well, Peru, Bolivia, Argentina, Paraguay, and even French Guiana. They might have left him there to rot, as they did—who was it, back then? Rat Man does not recall, but his history like his geography is emotional. There is only the awful mess of now, and everything else is the Dark Ages. To him, the Tropic of Cancer is that of rage, that of Capricorn is a steaming sulk. Paris is Orange is Lyon. The swine is everywhere, whizzing through people's heads like a fast silent movie, edited with care to be both barbaric and repetitious. Lest anyone forget.

How right, Rat Man thinks. Make us sick of him before cutting him in two. But don't do it until we've really had our fill. The expectation is all. I could hold the basket, release the blade, I could hold his mother down or back at the vital moment. No, the fatal, I should say. Help with the hosing-down afterward. Some wouldn't, they would want to peer at every last twitch when the amputated face appeared to be praying or smiling. No, when it is done, it's done. I am not one to linger on such things, goggling and gaping. I'd ask for the septum, of course. What is memory without a souvenir? I would in all probability be given his glasses, though, or their case. They tend to avoid the messy. They could do that beforehand too. A man going to the block doesn't need to look to find his way. They see to that. Nor would he be reading his mail or getting a speck of cinder out of a child's eye. The blur would help to fix his mind. So they could let me have them beforehand, still warm from his pocket, the bridge of his nose, the head hot with wondering what it was going to feel like in five minutes' time.

His abrupt rage at having conned himself the man was in Paris makes him more savage than he means to be. Yet, all considered, he has not exactly wasted the time. Wherever the prisoner is, he has also become a figure on the streets of Paris, indelibly linked with Rat Man too. And dealing with the treacherous Alphonse has been good practice. What he has not yet worked out is why this dreadful man, so well thought of, never reached the highest rank. The next worry after that, if he ever reaches it (he might never), is how so low-ranking an officer could have been responsible for such an atrocity. Answer: it was delegated down. The SS knew his zeal.

For now, he fumes and writhes, unable to lay a hand on his prey. Then he goes as soft and quiet as silk, teasing himself with a Latin American journey he will now not have to make. Not that he ever would have. He sees it, though, arriving at one blinding-white hotel after registering as Etienne Poulsifer, *Homme des Rats,* and overhearing the German spoken in the hallways. Cutting his initials with a piece of broken glass in the top of every bar. Enlisting all the rats south of the border to track the man down. Making phone calls, having breakfast in bed on a silver tray big enough to trot horses on. He lunches with the suave, learned one who collects blue eyes, turns down with an embarrassed smile an invitation to go swimming together. All I do is paddle, Rat Man says. The other whistles a tune from *Madama Butterfly* and mentions the pool he used to have at camp. At *camp?* Rat Man blinks. Where I worked, the other tells him. Never used. Never learned. Too busy to learn later in life. You have to come here to catch up with your childhood. Rat Man nods and says: Get it back somehow. Even if it breaks your neck to do it. If only Rat Man could swim, he would join this Mengele for a dip, pull him under and stuff the fox's head into his mouth, then wind the fur around his face, and hold him there on the bottom until he stopped shuddering. Then he could tread water in history as the man who killed Mengele, almost in the same league as— He tries to name the great assassins, but can't bring any to mind, and this gives him pause. If I don't know who's forgotten, he muses, I don't know who's remembered. Nobody knows who does all the forgetting or the remembering. Life and death are too anonymous for me. Give me something more personal, please.

Sharli pats his quivering thigh. They slink into bed together. She plays a tape of the sounds that jets make when landing. He can tell a jumbo from a DC-8. The Airbus is different again, as is the Caravelle. I'd be just as good as a blind man, he exclaims, with a little practice. I could be of use at night. I could tell them what is coming in. They already know what's coming in, she says, long before it's anywhere near the runway. You old fudge-pot. Now be quiet and push when I tell you to. As he does, he tells himself this is the life that everyone has. The life that *he,* in the St. Joseph jail, no longer has. Oh, he could shove it in between the bars, but the warders would club it down. Rat Man is virile again, and Sharli laments the wasted years. He is getting better the older he gets. Then they fall asleep without fear. Off to French Guiana with banjos. Bananas. Fried octopus. Flying fish. The heat of all the centuries beneath his jaw. By now, though, he knows excitement when he sees it.

Off to Lyon? she asks.

Wouldn't tell you if I was.

I'd be able to tell. Honest, it's the way you move your hands. You look clean through me, and I know.

A few trips, he tells her, in my mind. I'm going to stay in Paris. I'm Rat Man of Paris, not Lyon, or some other provincial place. This is the big league. I'm not going to start slumming now. I once lived in the provinces, and look where it got me. There are wolves and hippos who've had richer lives than mine. Apart from you and your marvelous handling of me, et cetera. I was once a kid. Now I'm done for. What was in between is like brown paper soaked in vinegar. Maybe I'd have been a good Nazi. Any blockhead can lug a bullwhip around. Yell. It would have been more interesting than getting killed. Half killed. All I can remember of my childhood before the awful things is nonstop piano music, scales and sonatas, going round and round like a music box with me inside it. Nice too. Ours was a house of music, the piano was always going. It made you wonder if there was anything outside the door but music. Open the door and you found another piano going like mad, with those tight little patterns from Bach, like a dozen children sucking bonbons fast. The only silence I ever knew, I think, was not when the music stopped, but the spaces in between the notes. Not much silence at all.

Wow, she tries to say, but it won't come out. Her mouth stays open, baying or yawning. He likes it that way, glistening vermilion. She looks very alive in there and it reminds him, it reminds him. He says so, and she laughs.

Mucous membranes. She says it to show them.

I haven't seen too much of them, he says. It's just as well. I'm sort of saved up. For somebody.

And we know who. She pouts, jealous.

The whole of Paris knows who. It's no secret by now. Nothing personal, Rat Man says brightly. It's the tempo of the times.

She winces at the cliché, as at Rat Man's new vision of himself as Someone. She too has seen the makeshift posters. The city is far from humming with the news, but a certain stir has begun. All Rat Man has to do is to somehow stir things up even more. Now, then, Poussif, she whispers, blowing bubbles into her *citron pressé* through the straw, let's forget about him for a while. He must have had a mother and a father. If they're still alive, and I doubt it, they ought to do some of the worrying. There are times when folk have to be left to their families to fuss about, even war criminals.

But she has not reckoned with Rat Man's intricate hold on the horrors of his past, or on the details of the criminal's arrival in France. Now he is animated for the first time since being a boy, no longer sleepwalking in a doldrum. Somehow he must not miss his moment, his cue. Not yet does he think of recent events as urging him toward his one and only destiny, as distinct from a quiet muddled life until the last prayer over his corpse, but he has begun to develop the idiom of self-importance. This does not cheapen or simplify him, but it makes him more tense, and a bit more abrupt with Sharli. His emotions have been given back to him, thawed out at room temperature, and he cannot resist them. Newborn, or reborn, he fondles in himself the small boy with a lust for blood.

Poussif no longer wins his attention; she has to call him Rat Man. Already he is planning in his impetuous way, determined now to install the Boche as a permanent presence in Paris. In spite of all geography, all trains, all local bylaws. He churns out posters and, in a fit of ingenuity, sets about acquiring an outfit similar to that in the newspaper photographs, all the way from the fedora hat to the pointed stylish shoes. Within a week he is ready to withstand her inspection in the tiny courtyard where he no longer grooms the pebbles. She cannot believe it. Even his face seems to match, though a trifle pudgier than that of the man at the café in Lima. But then, Rat Man is approximating an image from years ago. He is pudgier-faced than that one, but the man in jail right now is pudgier than he.

Twelve

Into the streets goes her ward and her lover, wheeling the ancient baby cart, within which he has stuffed the fox fur wrapped in a baby shawl. On both sides of the hood, and on the back, he has glued posters announcing that the man who wheels this effigy is an infamous war criminal guilty of burning babies. The placard hung over his chest from a cord round his neck announces the number of people whose lives he has ruined. 26,887. As he walks through an at least interested throng, he tries to envision that many people gathered together on a soccer field, say, but there is never enough room. He gets tired after the first hundred, who fill the netted space behind the goal, and begins to think lazily in thousands, an almost invisible number. So he takes it for granted that, milling around him, peering and jostling, at least twenty-six thousand eight hundred and eighty-eight approach him in the course of a week. Of course. Then he subtracts one as he warms to his work, half wondering why, in the midst of such a crowd, he still thinks he sees the little expatriate Spanish novelist observing his progress with an eye that gives nothing away. Should Rat Man accost him and ask something? Something mild and trivial? No, that would be to tamper, and if there is one thing Rat Man hates to tamper with it is an ongoing silence.

He teaches himself, through reviving caustic memories, to bring tears to his eyes on the spur of the moment, and at least a few of those who see him feel a pang. How can this hoax be moving? Clearly the criminal himself is a long way off, but this walkabout reminder is more real to them than any chubby, bespectacled bourgeois from the Automobile Club of La Paz. This is Rat Man's edge, and he knows it. There are no limits to this part he plays, so long as the police do no more than move him on, which is exactly what he intends doing anyway. From place to place he goes, never so much as smiling, but doing an ashamed weep at the crucial places. Now he bronzes his face with boot polish to simulate a tan acquired beneath the Latin American sun. He no longer buffs his heels, which, from each full day's trudging, split wide open. Sharli chides him, buffs him herself, then gives up; he won't hold still, he has begun to fidget and flinch. He wants to be out there, even at night, with an old bicycle lamp on the baby carriage, and out he goes.

He has taken his own place on the boulevards. Rat Man has supplanted himself. Now he broadens out the show, each day, with sound effects. A scratchy tape of "Deutschland über Alles" plays as he plods through the spaces they make to let him through. It should be against the law, but it is only contrary to good taste. Some sneer. Some run up and jostle him, try to tip the fox-baby from its cot on wheels. A good sign, this, because it means the illusion has begun to bite. They all know better, Rat Man knows. I know better myself. Two helium balloons with skull and crossbones now fly from the top of the hood or canopy, popped once or twice a week by pranksters with cigarettes. Try as he does in his limited off-duty time, he cannot find a Nazi uniform, but he has not yet approached the theaters, where surely a property man as willing as an Alphonse can rummage around and come up with the right combination of field gray, leather, and bullwhip. He corrects himself: the SS wore black, with white shirts, and their badges of rank were different. He resolves to make the illusion authentic. All he needs is money, and money is coming in, clanking or fluttering into the humble basket nestled on the rainproof cover that hides the baby's legs. He dreams of designing a new game called the War Criminal Execution Kit, complete with guillotine, war criminal with detachable head, and such extras as a black blindfold, a bottle of fake blood, and a small typed notice to display outside the nonexistent prison wall. Too much trouble. He leaves such things to his imitators, who will come after him, long after he has retired to his rebuilt native village, quitting Paris, the scene of his triumph, just to get some peace and quiet, away from the television cameras, the newspaper interviewers, the incessant acclaim of street people, who all remember him as the force that beefed up a life sentence into an execution.

To his regalia he adds a toy drum, which he taps with a gong hammer found in the debris in the Street of the Cat Who Fishes. This works well, better even than the German anthem. He alternates the two. First the drum as he walks, then the anthem as he pauses to get his breath and his bearings. Then the drum again as the tape ends and clicks. But still he does not use the Boche's name. Now he decides he was right all along. As a walking effigy likely to be photographed at any moment, he embodies thousands of the damned rather than the man tossed out of Bolivia on the whim of the regime in power.

Lashed to the insides of his knees, two cymbals clash when he pauses and knocks his knees together or grate silently amid the buzz of traffic when he walks ahead. He mostly forgets to halt and make the cymbals sound.

As he looks down into the baby carriage, he marvels at how lucky he is; the fox's face brings that of a charred baby to mind, especially as from Sharli's collection he has filched a pale blue ribbon to wind around the head. Like a fallen halo. He readjusts the shawl, of course, but makes sure that the ribbon shows. To his outfit he adds a homemade Nazi armband, with the swastika back to front, but no one notices or cares. The effect is undeniable. The faded gray suit works well too, seemingly so far from atrocity, but all the more telling for that; the mass murderer is on his way to a cocktail party, or has just come from one. This is the man-about-town who burns the town, the boulevardier who makes the boulevards run with blood. He adds blood to his image, each day daubing lipstick on his hands before going out.

Here he comes, at a distance of some twenty meters. First they hear the drum, which stops. Then the raucous anthem. He still is some distance away behind a throng of people with nothing better to do. The skull-and-crossbones balloons float above the heads. Now he lumbers through, wheeling the carriage as if it were a tumbril, but it is not that heavy. In good daylight the hands blaze almost orange. He bangs the drum, making a child's noise that half summons the well-to-do to dinner. As they look into the interior and gasp at the black, hard, tiny face, he starts the tape, does a mock *Heil* with the drumming hand, sometimes forgetting to put down the drumstick. They read all the placards, the message across his chest. As the red hand rises in the hated salute, they whistle or boo, jeer, and hiss. Some laugh outright, glad to have survived into posthistory. Some laugh because they have not the faintest idea of what is going on. They have never even heard of Rat Man, but they are the minority. Usually, the excited whisper precedes him by five minutes.

Rat Man is coming! And he always comes, with drum and balloons and blunt placards among the equally blunt signs that say *Presse* or *Eau de Boyer,* or scream *Qui veut tuer Paris?* No one wants to kill Paris, he thinks, but only Rat Man wants to liven it up. Can he get into the Métro and install his show in the space reserved for *mutilés de guerre?* Hardly. Too much trouble. This is the City of Light, and famous as such, and he is the hand of darkness marching through it with a plea for justice. Sometimes a sidewalk cleaner precedes him on a mild-mannered motorcycle with the sign *Clean Sidewalks!* on its rear. He tromps past Burger Kings, accordion players, old- and new-style pissoirs, the former like some soup kitchen left over from World War One, the latter like the rear end of a hyper-modern train. He enters neither, knowing that his baby carriage would vanish and, within an hour, show up in a suburb. So, he has cut down on his intake of liquid. He cannot see himself asking someone to mind his baby while he goes to relieve himself. No one obliges a war criminal. If, he thinks, there is truly a legend of Paris, banal enough to darken the City of Light with slogans as crass as "The gendarme has become a motorcycle ace" and "The newspaper crier dreams in his plastic booth," then there is a place for Rat Man. Thus. "Rat Man once more roams the boulevards, with timely reminders." Who are Jacques Brel, Pierre Cardin, Catherine Deneuve, Nastassja Kinski, and Yves Montand? Nameless names, blank as the identity of the envisioned assassin of Paris. *Qui veut tuer Paris?* Well, Rat Man will kill it with conscience if they let the criminal loose to write his memoirs in Lausanne, only nominally jailing him. He bows his head low over the fox-baby's head, awaiting the blade.

He only just notices the air. The weather here is a touch sharper now, which invigorates him and increases the pace of his stroll as he walks his baby. Rats were never this good. On warmer days, after some worried thought, he stalks out in an old shirt from which he has torn the collar. Around his neck he daubs a bright band of scarlet to mark the cut of honor. This prediction-aftermath pleases him a lot. If only he could somehow carry a head cradled in his arm. But the baroque puts him off. He does not want to add unnecessarily to his tableau. Unless a helper comes along. Not Sharli, who is revolted, but maybe Alphonse? Not the real one, but someone like him? A cooperative liar of almost any stripe. No. Rat Man sees the whole thing getting out of hand.

So, at least in his mind, he goes the other way. Just one balloon, then? Yes. He sticks to the drum, but junks the tape. At night, however, he arranges candles on a plate, fixing their bottoms to it with hot wax, and arranges this on top of the hood, as if (he hopes) he were bearing an altar before him in memory of the dead, the maimed, the deported. The final effect evokes Christmas, however, and is not stern enough by half, so he abandons it. In the course of a week, in which he has not slept for the ferment in his head, he makes a dozen changes, using whatever material is at hand. Small chairs from his doll's house appear on the hood, mysteriously occupied by faint figures made of fuzz. Then they go. Now he blows up and bangs a paper bag, but the bang is hardly audible in all the commotion. The police seem inexplicably in sympathy with him. When he peddled his rats, they were much more hostile, but that was in the leaner days when no one cared, when no one had anything to care about. While it stays fresh, he holds a rabbit's heart in his mouth, tiny and slimy, but he sometimes likes to talk, to answer a question or two, and the heart gets in the way. He respects himself, though, for being willing to give his all to this act. He wants results. To an inquiring reporter, he says, after much laborious thought: *Never let anything get away until it begins to come after you.*

If he could only come up with fifty more, he would have a collection of *pensées,* worthy of being passed out in the street by eminent philosophers themselves going mad or blind. But he rarely gets ideas. When he has a moment alone, dreaming fondly of Sharli sleek in her long nightdress, which she calls her strawberry-swan suit for the emblem at its neck, he remarks only the new speed his heart has gained. It never slows. He breathes too fast. His hands feel clammy. His nose bleeds, but not predictably enough to be useful. His feet are killing him, the heels most of all; the calluses have split wide open, bleed all the time into his socks, and will soon need surgery. He sees his new career coming to an end, after which he will have to wheel the carriage around on crutches, or, worse, while walking on his knees, with his nose nudging the crossbar of the handles. So, if he took a week off and got himself spruced up, wouldn't that be wise? It would, but he would lose momentum. The crowds would find something else to divert them.

Or, on the other hand, might they cheer him on his return, and swarm about him even more? Absence makes the mob grow fonder. He does not believe it. He cannot let go, not even for a day or two. Almost a physical wreck, he still feels sturdy-minded. Strong enough to see this thing through to its unknown end, with the Spanish novelist logging his every motion, his every grimace, only to write him up at a later date under an assumed name: the name of a character, like Don Quixote, whom no one ever knew. He dithers, locks his fingers and cracks his knuckles. The lipstick will not wash off, at least not under the feeble pressure of the tap outside. His hands look chapped, uncared for throughout a severe winter, but Rat Man knows better. Sharli has stockpiles of unperfumed cold cream, with which he now lards his heels, and then he feels them sliding around in his socks as if he were walking sideways as well as forward.

If this is a crisis in what he now regards as his performance, then the only thing is to soldier on as if no crisis existed. If anything breaks, it will not be he. He longs to sit with Sharli in her car under the big wash of the jets, but he cannot spare the time. At first he did only four hours a day, but now he does not only nights but, with an aching head and legs of jelly, the small hours, which give him a different clientele, rowdier, nastier, altogether more dangerous. They shove him, mock him, pop the solitary balloon, but he gets a brighter lamp to walk with, and that seems to tone them down. In these hours, and he is grateful, he can sometimes be seen shoving forward entirely alone, not even bothering to pound his drum, and beginning to shiver. The rain has done its work on him. The fox-baby is always damp now, and his shoes are white with mold at the welts. The fedora hat protects him, of course, but it has shrunk, and he has to stretch it each morning with both hands, then jam it hard onto his head. Sometimes he yearns for the seedy haven of the Street of the Cat Who Fishes, or even the cell of the criminal from Bolivia, Peru, or wherever it was he came from. He too would like to be tubby and shortsighted at the unvarnished table in St. Joseph. The baby butcher. The flogger. The incinerator of the old. Just to be as comfortable as he, being fed at regular intervals. True, Sharli at regular intervals leaves a bag of provisions just inside his drawbridge door, but she never finds him in. The only place to find him is in the streets, doing his slow-motion walk with failing zeal, but doing it as he must until the very flesh drops away, and only a skeleton wheels his carriage. Perhaps that is the awesome, ghastly combination he wants to achieve. When she tracks him down, he merely shakes his head, but she has not yet found him in the early-morning hours, when he is perhaps the loneliest figure in the city, wheeling his vengeance through the empty streets, among rats no longer his and refuse uncollected. He needs a sign, a call, a death. Only then can he give over. By then he will be very old, able only to mumble and shuffle, needing artificial tears to keep his eyes moist.

Hold on now, says the interviewer on the street. Just be yourself—cameras know nothing.

After a few false starts, they get going, and Rat Man takes a deep breath almost as if to smell his own presence from the surrounding street. He explains about the atrocity in the village, then tells less well about the years in between, which refuse to come into focus.

From pillar to post, he says, from job to job. Some days I didn't know my own name. I half wished they'd branded me with a number so that I could look at my arm to check. A man ought not to feel like a jam or a bun. He looks all right, they'd say, what's he making a big fuss about? The war is over. We won. Let all that stuff flow past. I did. Then it came back and sort of encircled me. I was an island in the muck. Sure, I made ends meet. Poor, slovenly jobs you wouldn't ask an ape to do. But jobs. I used to try and recall my parents' faces, but they had no faces for me. All I saw was flames. If you can see a howl, I saw howls. The amazing thing is, I'm still here. I escaped, but I couldn't escape from the consequences of it all. In the end I became Rat Man of the boulevards. It was something to enjoy doing. I made friends. A few coins came my way. It got me out in the fresh air. I was more or less healthy from walking my rat around.

It was not always, monsieur, a rat?

Dumb or in some cases quite eloquent animals.

Quite eloquent, you say? The interviewer presses him.

A squirrel is eloquent, in my book. Your chimp doesn't do badly either. Rat Man smiles, chimp or squirrel.

Squirrels and chimpanzees. But nowadays—

Ah, Rat Man sighs, what I'm using now, for a rather different end, is a fox fur—a family heirloom, a treasure you might say, handed down, and lovingly picked up. I wouldn't be without it.

So, between 1944 and now, which is a long time, you have made do. Have you been happy during this time?

I found love, Rat Man says quietly. Without that, you might as well chew nails. My Sharli wasn't always there, oh no, but for the past few years . . . One day I'll make it up to her, I've had to neglect her. What with my duties in the streets, and such.

You now address yourself, in this highly theatrical fashion, to the recently arrived Butcher of Lyon. Do you think Parisians care?

Thousands, at least several hundred a day, cheer me on. I know what they want. They know what they want. His head on a pike somewhere near the Arc de Triomphe. What about you, sir? Any little I can do to speed that up, wherever he is, I am willing to go without sleep to do it.

You blame him for the death of your parents? Rat Man agrees, and cites various numbers. A shock follows.

The ex-Nazi in question was not responsible. True, he was responsible for much, and for that he will be tried in due course, but the destruction of your native village, monsieur, was none of *his* doing.

That's a lie, Rat Man gasps. A bloody fib. Are you trying to make a mug of me? His face is aflame. And yet, such is his need, his rage, that even in the midst of yet another mistake, he gropes at straws. If the man he wanted was never in Paris, but in Orange and Lyon, then maybe the one he really wants has been in Paris all along? Never mind how he mislocates and misidentifies, history remains the same. Certain things were done to him, and undone they cannot be. Lies, he croaks. Nothing but lousy, collaborationist lies. Are you really trying to make a mug of me, at *my* time of life?

Only to the extent that you may be trying to make mugs of us. You have the wrong Nazi, monsieur. Honestly. *That* man has never been found.

I'll take any Nazi I can, Rat Man tells the world. You needn't be too particular. They have more in common with one another than they don't. What I do is in part symbolic, see.

So you would advocate guillotining any representative figure? Is that civilized? What if—

Who's civilized? Rat Man becomes agitated and his jowls begin to work. He does not believe what the man has said. He lacks the equipment to register it. As far as he is concerned, his rats were all one rat. The fox fur is another rat. The plastic ones were live. It makes no difference. He thinks in categories; a childhood trauma has made him think this way. He tries to explain this, half expecting two goons to arrive with a straitjacket and a hypo full of tranquilizer. But no, they would grab him and inject him only after the cameras had gone.

Life bleak, he says. Head full. Heart skips a beat. Then catches up. Nowhere to go. No folks. Not so much brought up as cuffed up. It turns you off. They look away. Look at that. He's not human. See how he rolls about. Make a living somehow. Pound the sidewalk. Keep your mouth shut. Show your rat. Shove off. Lick out empty cans. Chew offal. Drink from the tap. No wine, it kills my sense of proportion. Mooch from here to anywhere. Have no name. No number. Door opening funny upward. I'd fit in a fort. Pâté and bread if lucky. Bread if not. If doomed, only what cats bring in. My skull aches. I am what has come to be known as a parallel man.

The interviewer merely jabs the microphone nearer to Rat Man's mouth, which winds him up again, delighted to be heard, to be seen while being *heard out.*

That is to say, monsieur, someone very nearly not of this world, who looks like just about everyone else, but has very few connections with how they live their lives. I might be a reflection. An echo. A carbon copy. One of those xerox copies I use. I pass for human but I'm stunted. Not dangerous, or even clever; but sort of terminally buggered about. To no good purpose. But, if you put it the other way round, who would ever do the rat on the streets if it weren't for the likes of me? Needing me, they would never find me. The Street of the Cat Who Fishes. That is not so much an address, monsieur, as a hole in the human condition. I slink in and shut up. I love to shut up. I never need to see myself, not even in a small piece of broken mirror. A reflection doesn't need to look at himself. He knows. I know my Paris, though. Look at these heels. He shows them both: the scabs combining, the silt of blood and filth all the way to the arches. That's what you get for combing Paris for a few people of good conscience. Nazis? It's not so much Nazis I want as fellow monsters. Each time I wake, I am glad I cannot see my face. I turn it out to face the world, and I bring it home each day like a whipped dog.

The interviewer has run out of time, and goes, but Rat Man walks away, wheeling his pram, talking to them all for the first time in many years. They follow him, not so much listening as waiting for something awful to happen. His socks are in his pocket, but his shoes are on. He wheels around as if to catch an urchin spying on him, but he wants to catch the eye of the novelist behind him, noting and annotating him, and he does indeed think he sees him dodging out of sight into a tobacco store. The witnesses have gathered. He has been heard. Sharli will see him on the pearly screen, if they use the footage. He doubts it. He is tactless. A bungler with the wrong Nazi. Or so they say. He just knows, however, that this must be the man. We have found almost all of them now. To show them how humble he is, he walks on his knees, through puddles and mud. He takes the pram handle between his teeth and urges it forward. They cheer. He stands, clashes his knees, hastily inflates a new balloon, removes the placard from his breast and holds it aloft, turning through a full circle so that all can see. He isn't going to back down now. Some people think the world of him already. He can tell that. They want to see what he will do next. He has no program, he makes it up as he goes along, much as the Almighty did. But he will not rest, not until the cell in St. Joseph is empty and hosed down. He has already forgotten, or set aside, his having fixed on the wrong man.

Sing for us, Rat Man. The cry reaches him from as far away as Bordeaux, but they want him to sing.

Not a song left in me. I'll drum, though. He starts a tattoo, makes it faster as he advances, and taps the balloons with the drumstick out of something close to exuberance. He has been interviewed by TV, something he has always turned his back upon, and it feels as if someone has removed his facial skin, like one of those plastic masks. He no longer feels his own man, but co-opted by the big league of life, by those who count. Worries nibble at him. Was he dignified? Did he speak clearly? How did he look? Human or apelike? Most of all, did he look like the man in question, who may well see the newsreel in his cell? What a thought. If Rat Man has impersonated him right, the man will see something like his own ghost advancing upon him out of history with drum, balloon, pram, and fedora. If he dies of shock, Rat Man will have cheated Madame Guillotine without meaning to. He shrugs, shudders, freezes.

No more interviews. God alone knows how even this one will end up. Better to skulk in the streets until the glorious day long awaited. Taken short, with very few around him, he decides not to risk leaving the pram behind while he enters the *vespasienne* and, discreetly hunching forward, unbuttons his out-of-date pants and relieves himself into the bottom of the ancient carriage, holding the cover up with one hand while masking his parts with the drum. Should the police catch him at this, the whole enterprise would flop. Too laughable by far. No one comes or sees, and now he wheels the thing forward again, hearing the liquid slosh around in the rusted bottom, and noting a trail of it leaking away behind him. Yes, he remembers, as with bombers in the war: I could rig up a little hose from me into the pram, and no one would be any the wiser. You have to have your creature comforts when you're on the road.

When Sharli catches up with him, about two in the morning, outside Les Halles, whose colonnades resemble white rolltop desks, everyone is too busy to notice a mere Rat Man. Hardly anyone is there, and certainly no one who, like Sharli, has seen him shown up on TV, slithering from one bungle to another. He passes unremarked, uncared about, an old ghost wheeling cauliflowers to and fro, or hoping to steal a sack of potatoes. He sees her at last, puts on his tough and furtive face, which she cannot see; but she lays a hand on him, as it were touching the whole of his being with it, tosses the drumstick away with a frail clatter, hauls down the balloon, and begins to steer him home. A long walk, and wordless too.

If only, he wishes, I could just climb into this pram and sleep all the way home. Do I say this or just think it? His legs hover, going nowhere, and when Sharli grabs his arm to hold him up he feels light as fish bone, and less sleek.

Thirteen

His eyes have quit. He senses he is going to fall, or fall away, even from her clasp. This she senses as well and hugs him tighter only to feel she is going to slither off the surface of the planet after him. Her hold slackens, but he squeezes her more tightly, telling her to renew it. His hat falls off. He burrows his face down into her shoulder, smothering a sob of fatigue, loneliness, and littleness. They sway as if to music, grave and slow. The battery in the bicycle lamp on the pram begins to flag. The white of the bulb yellows. And still they do not move along, almost as if standing on a plank in pitch dark. He knows now that, if he does not go home to her, then he goes home to a hell of his own devising, for which no Boche can be held responsible.

Now, she tells him.

No. He cannot move. His legs have locked, his heels feel like cement. She shoves, she heaves. He does not even falter. So she hugs him again. He is not ready. Red-letter days are exhausting. She has forgotten which day this is. He has been on the loose too long. Paris has had its share, and so has the Boche in Lyon. Even as she urges him once again, soothing him with a coo-sound, she sees something flutter in the shadows. A cape flicking about. An odd-looking hat. A glint of something, surely not a sword. Surely she does not see the Hispanic face, well razored by the steadiest of hands. Rat Man utters a magnanimous-sounding sigh and sinks to the ground in spite of her arms. Down she goes with him, thinking his heart has given way at last. Not yet. He is murmuring, grunting, and his jaw, his shirt, are wet with blood. Something in him has exploded. Her calls become a series of accelerating screams, but there is no longer any shape out there in the shadows. No motion. She pats Rat Man and dabs his face, but this sets him groaning, as if through imperfect anesthesia. Legs splayed wide, he leans over, ducking his jaw at regular intervals for reasons unknown. By the light of the lamp, dim as it is, she now sees the big blotch on one cheek, the smaller blotch on the other. From side to side she swings the lamp, inspecting him, and then begins to scream again. Had he not been shot, she would have thought some skewer had passed through his face and then withdrawn. The blood is copious, he cannot talk, but he refuses to lie down. Yes, she thinks, they took him in his sleep, just as they took him once before in the deep sleep of childhood. The police car is a long time coming, and the gendarmes are much too placid. He will live, of course. They speed away, horn blasting the weird plaintive multiple toot that says grace nonstop, while Rat Man sits erect, his knee cymbals exactly mated, one handkerchief to his left cheek, which he himself holds, the other on the other, pressed firm by Sharli, shot through the cheeks while yawning, in the twentieth century of his life.

III
Sharli

Fourteen

In the light of the emergency room she sees again the two blotches. He must have had his mouth open, says the young doctor; otherwise the shot would have removed his jaw. The bullet passed clean through the flesh of both cheeks. Unpleasant but far from fatal. We'll patch him up in no time. He won't be able to talk without pain, but there is more blood than damage. Now one of the policemen asks what she saw, and she mentions a shadow. He always thought someone was following him around—a little expatriate Spanish novelist. Can you imagine anything more unlikely? Oh, fanatics come in all shapes and sizes, they reassure her. She gives them Rat Man's version since he is unable to talk, and they promise to do a composite. Unfortunately, the composite will fit several thousand Parisians. But the police will try. It is all too calm for her. Had Rat Man been dead, they would have shown more interest; as it is, the shooting is a novelty. They seem to know who he is, a bum of the boulevards. Such characters go to waste all the time, very few of them so neatly holed.

They were trying to kill him, then?

Good or bad marksman, they pronounce, he must have had a silencer. They will hunt for the spent bullet in the daylight. Or even sooner, depending.

And if you find it?

From where he fell it must have been fifty meters to the nearest cover. Anyone using a pistol for such a shot was not aiming to shoot him clean through the cheeks. Whereas, with a rifle, yes. There are those among us, madame, who accept potluck with their shooting. If the round kills, well, O.K. If not, an effect has been made anyway. Some warnings are lethal.

So you think he was asking for it, parading around as a war criminal? He even made it to the newsreels.

They know who he is, not only Rat Man but Rat Man the ex-Nazi impostor. Did he never think, they ask her, of all the right-wing fanatics left over from God knows how many wars? Just as there are hundreds of reasons for leaving him alone as an eccentric, a holy fool, a tourist draw, there are hundreds of reasons for polishing him off. In the twisted mind, she hears, logic is very personal. He will recover soon. The wounds are of the flesh only.

Aren't they all? She has begun to weep, but Rat Man sits there with stony serenity, in pain, but showing little of what he feels. His mind has not ceased to work, she can see that. But he looks almost gratified, as if, through some such twisted logic as the police have just mentioned, his being shot by an unknown assailant amounts to beheading the Boche in Lyon.

Not of the bone, the sinew, the muscle, the vital organ, the brain, they tell her in a hasty mouthful. She knows, but the only alternatives she can think of to flesh wounds are those of the mind. Rat Man is thinking how exquisite her schoolteacher's handwriting is: ample, curly, honest and emphatic, like a crop growing among the lines of the pages she covers when preparing her lessons. Even if, from now on, she deals with him only by letter, poste restante of course, that will be enough. The pram, the balloon, the lamp, the fox fur, are where they left them. Presumably. Like something omitted from a flea market. Someone else can wheel the pram about, pound the drum, float the balloon, flick on the tape. The bloodstained placard from his chest is already in the hospital incinerator, but it might have been part of the evidence. Vaguely he wonders why whoever it was did not shoot him in the chest, the heart, with on a clear night that big white piece of cardboard to aim at, as with a firing squad. I was a good target, he decides. So you can see how deliberate they were. It was the face they wanted. Yet my face, unlike the rest of me, never resembled *him.* So they were not shooting him in effigy. They were shooting me as Rat Man. That is what comes of being interviewed in the street. At least I have my jaw and will not have to be fed through a tube for the rest of my days. I'll put aside my props. Life is serious from now on. Rat Man has made his point. And so have they. I just wonder if he in the St. Joseph got wind of me and hired someone to do it. Or did they do it without any prompting from him? It hurts, but it doesn't hurt as much as you'd expect. It's not like being shot through the cheeks in childhood. Then the cheeks are smaller. More delicate. The jaw is nearer, isn't it? But who would shoot a pretty, anyway? He knows an answer to that, and he knows who would set fire to one too. Would I, he thinks, have been better off shot back then? Like some others? No, who wants a maimed child? Who even wants to hose down a child with a hole through his chops? I'd have been put in a jar for experts to look at. They might have sold me to one of those tribes that skewer themselves, so I'd fit in better. The city will do me fine. It doesn't matter what you look like so long as the approximation is human. They're cruel in the countryside, oh yes; but in the city you can get away with something like one-third visibly human, that's all they ask. In fact they prefer it that way because there's less of you to think about, to consider. It's full-blooded humans that waste city folk's time. We float on cities like lilies on water.

He can go home, they say. He cannot remember where to go. It must be the painkiller. He feels like a dunce, as previously when Sharli lured him to the tennis court, and he stood with racket in hand, utterly uninterested in the ball she patted over the net to him. He watched it rise and fall, then come to a halt, but without the slightest desire to do anything to it. It has always been like this. He likes the movements of a soccer ball, but has no thoughts of ever touching it. When, in the Luxembourg Gardens, a child's ball rolled toward him, he watched it exhaust its energy, and then looked away. Never in his life has he rolled a ball back to a child, afraid no doubt that its motion, so much like that of the planet he rides upon, will give him vertigo. He loves to see things stop. He loves organ music, especially in churches, but he dotes on the moment when it halts and all he hears is the majestic echo, which then yields to whispers and to the untidy sounds of birds.

You can go, they tell him. Sharli tells him, but where is her car? The police take them both along, back to the place where he was shot, near Les Halles, no longer a scene of frantic activity. No longer do night-owling dandies sip cognac with butchers in bloodied aprons, but tonight, Rat Man thinks, he might see just such folk. No. The old market is an enormous garden, and all the animal-vegetable commotion has shifted to a site near Orly. Of course. The pram and its trappings have vanished, stolen by kids, he is sure of that. Then let them play. They will light a fire in its belly and roast chestnuts. With powerful beams of light, the police begin searching for the bullet as he and Sharli drive away gently so as not to jar him.

Back at the site, apart from the police combing the walls

with their searchlights, there is no sign of his having been there at all.

Already his mind has moved onward. Writing on a small pad beneath which he keeps his right thigh rigid, he lists the places he would like to see as a wounded tourist:

Pont Neuf, where peddlers used to defecate on the bridge.

Place de la Concorde, where Du Barry screamed and plunged on her way to the guillotine.

One more, he scrawls. The statue of Balzac, where the whores collect.

She is astounded he has the energy, but she does not know this is the beginning of his farewell to Paris, a farewell after which he does not have to leave, but a farewell to one way of looking at the city. He is no longer going to float, to wander. He may just depart, he may just stay. A man shot through the cheeks, and wadded speechless, need not commit himself, especially on paper. Various destinies await him, neither sordid nor splendid, but humdrum without being banal. That is how he sees it. A man whose life, whose jaw anyway, has been saved because he happened to be yawning when the bullet passed through him, entitles himself to freedom of choice. And not only that. He entitles himself to vagary, caprice, and whim. If, amid the catastrophes of daily life, he does better just by being careless than by being prudent, he has earned a certain freedom of action.

He cannot even mouth his sentiments, but he gestures them to her even as she makes him swallow the second painkilling pill. He gathers up the world in his arms and hugs it to him as he nods at her. Then he throws it upward as an armful of flowers and watches the stems land higgledy-piggledy on the well-vacuumed rug. He pats his chest. He leans gravely forward and pats her pubic patch.

Is that a promise? She half begins to laugh.

He nods, then shakes his head. The shake of his head answered her half-laugh, she thinks. Out of all this mess, he has made something happen. Actually, he made many things happen. Can it be that, instead of justice, he wanted only recognition? Not from me. From Paris. From even a neo-Nazi assassin. Does that abolish his childhood, the in-between years of sleepwalk trauma? Does that lay his ghosts to rest? Will he now, as he puts his head beside me on the pillow, wheeze ever so finely through both cheeks? She stops that dead. Rat Man, *mon p'tit Poussif,* as she calls him now, has re-won his dignity overnight. Only the doll's house remains among the mildewed newspapers in the hovel on the tiny street off the Rue de la Huchette, where angled timbers hold up half the houses. Funny, names. My parents tried to call me Chelsea after honeymooning in London. I was conceived in Chelsea. Now I am Sharli. What will I be tomorrow. Sharli and Poussif. The phrase has a comfortable sound. He will sift the pebbles in the patio all over again. He will no longer turn his back on the television. Not now that he has been intimate with it. He will read. I will bring him up, and out of it. Menton next summer.

But: will they shoot him again?

Not as long as he desists. He can be Rat Man, but he must never again be the Boche's double. No, she decides, I don't want him to be Rat Man either. I want him to retire. He will design doll houses. Is he going to fuss about the fox fur? Wherever it is now. Almost all of what little he had he needs no longer. He has come out the other end. I am with child.

Rat Man is watching her closely, gesturing now and then: a wave, one-handed; a silent applause, with two; a caution expressed with a wagging finger and one eye squinted as he makes his head sag sideways. Lord God, she frets, will he want to go on television again, now that he's news? By the time he talks again, perhaps he won't be. The papers will report it, but he'll be able to say nothing at all.

She is wrong. They all track him down, on the strict understanding—Sharli's Law—that he make no attempt to speak. He gestures, though. He nods. All of Paris sees his still or moving picture within a couple of days. And his wounds. He shows his heels again, much cleaned up. Most of all, he is a sight, only slightly less silent than when he wandered the streets. He wanders them again, trailed by cameras and cables, flash photographers and half-incredulous fans. Rat Man has been shot! *Paris-Match* captures him for inclusion among stories about people he thinks his ancestors must have known, whereas he does not; their names arouse a tremor only, of subdued familiarity, as if he has been born again without quite losing the echoes of that other life. He puffs his chest. He accepts the new clothes. Gifts arrive. Copperplate letters of sympathy. By registered mail comes a fox fur, not his own, but an uncannily close sibling. He accepts it. For a week the headlines own him while Sharli relates his story to the class he once addressed. In a strange blasted peace, he sits in Sharli's apartment and, with sympathetic amazement, on the screen that several times has borne his own face watches evening television with Sharli: *Jackie and Sara; Dallas; The Madman of the Desert;* Yehudi Menuhin playing Bach and Bartók; *Musiclub;* and *Flash 3.* The inside of his head is awash with light. Véronique and Davina do aerobics at his command on the *Gym Tonic* show, not that he would dream of attempting such exertions himself. Still, he consoles himself, a dying man can always learn a dead language. He *should.*

Then the furor begins to wane. If he wants more attention, he has to do something about it. He does not a jot. Sharli relaxes at last. No more rats. No more pram. No more drum, balloon, no more Boche. He settles in quite well, keeping his toothbrush—as yet unused because of his wounds—well apart from hers and going to enormous lengths to let her sleep since he needs less rest than she, and watches the screen until it stutters on to empty.

No more autographs. He begins to talk again.

The little Hispanic face no longer hovers behind him. How could it? He has nowhere to go to be followed to. The little lame novelist has gone back to work.

The police fail to find the bullet and keep on drawing

blanks. Person or persons unknown, they say. It may take years. Since the shooting, eight other people have been wounded, three killed. The Seine flows down to the sea. He hates apartment life. Feet marching above him. Stereos pounding through the neighbor walls. The whole building vibrates from the accumulated racket and, one day soon, when the exact frequency comes up, will crumble into dust. He would rather, he thinks, be lying in a plowed October field, under an incontinent horse, for a month, than have strangers tromping above him, turning up the bass on either side, filling the hallways with thunder much as all and sundry fill up his tiny street with trash.

No, he decides. Under the jets, yes. In a tent at the soccer ground, yes. Back in the Street of the Cat Who Fishes, of course. I cannot abide the vibrations of others. The doll's house is here, and that is a help; but a man cannot stagnate around his one and only possession, plus a magnifying glass, some crumbling newspapers, a newfangled fox fur, and the memory of a burning village. Now he longs for the frayed tape measure he'd wrapped around his thumb. When was that? In which life? Perhaps a bedtime story, told by day, would soothe him just enough. Or a rosebush to fuss. Yellow or white. Lavender, even.

The bell rings. The police have found and brought his pram, minus the balloon, the top cover. He motions them to take it away again. They refuse and leave it in the hallway. He makes another gesture, meaning he is going to make water into it, but they understand none of that. Minus one wheel, it can sit, it is hardly an heirloom. He wonders which babies sat and gurgled in it between 1914 and 1983. Should he and Sharli ever have the beginnings of a family, this thing would never do. Something much superior would sit in the hall, chained to the door lest the neighbors take it in like an orphan.

Fifteen

In the same mental breath, however, he thinks things so appalling he wishes he would never think again. This is the end. Rat Man has had his day. Paris needs him no more. What next, then? He needs no pram, no trappings, just enough energy to stay awake when they park under the glide path as in the good old times before the Boche.

And Sharli will stir him from his doze with what she says so brightly each morning to her pupils: *Bonjour, mes élèves!* and they chant a greeting in unison back to her, which overlaps in his head with someone reading aloud the names of the missing in action. Where was that? When? Has he just been through a war? A war has wounded him. A private, exhausting war based like so many wars on a total misunderstanding.

She watches him closely, noting that his eyebrows seem

more ruffled than usual when he wakes, as if tiny insects have frolicked along them in the night.

Flesh wounds, he tells her, cannot harm the soul, whereas vice versa . . . His speech is slurred and squeaky.

She agrees, knowing how you really wound the soul, with the image of a long-forgotten Nazi, who arrives slumped in a free seat in a DC-8. Thousands of lives fill with turmoil. Passions once in motion move themselves, she belatedly answers him, having nodded at what he said about flesh wounds without putting into words what she thought at that instant.

He does not understand at all, and assumes this is something she tells her classes. He takes it on trust. Up he gets, rummages in her closet, and emerges with two head-sized cardboard boxes, into which he shoves his hands. Now he does a dumb show, waving the boxes about as if signaling. That's how clumsy I feel, he says with forlorn fury. All I need is one for my head and I'll be set for life. For the rest of it. Talking thickly.

She walks across the living room and flips the TV on. Invited to watch, he smiles in his dreary way, then, with an almost frisky coquettish walk, hastens to watch the screen, mocking his motion as he goes. She has seen him do much the same in the street, after the shooting at least, when he wraps his arm around a lamppost, slow-motion, and tugs his sleeve straight with the other hand. A pointless, showy thing to do, it wins him a little attention from passersby, to whom he delivers always the same ravished smile, as if they have applauded him for some feat of conjuring. Didn't they always?

Yes, he tells her, I'm putting an arm around Paris. I'm being friendly, see.

It's been friendly to you. She sounds bitter.

Then, he answers, I'm just wasting a bit of my life where I've prospered. You have to take the rough with the smooth. Like the Boche. He had his good times, and soon they will slice through every blood vessel in his neck. Rat Man only guesses at the law, in this as well.

She knows he is wrong about the guillotine, but she knows better than to quarrel. Once upon a time, having been deafened by all that stereo music from neighboring apartments, she decided to get her own back, waiting until everything was quiet and then turning up her own stereo full blast; but no one seemed to notice. No one banged on the wall or came to the door to complain. Well, she decides, Poussif is just like that. You can't get through. The noise in his head is the noise in his head. He doesn't hear me when I tell him the guillotine is a thing of the past. He got the wrong man anyway. In the wrong place. God help us if they ever find the man he really wants. We'll have to leave the city and go live in Addis Ababa, some place like that, with no newspapers, no radio. Is Addis really like that or have they brought it up to date? I don't *care.* I just don't want any more *incidents.*

Lo, and behold Rat Man, she thinks. Look at him. As done for as the Shah of Iran. All he needs to perk him up is a future. All his future needs is a future. How do I build that for him? He won't build it himself, that's for certain. I am always with child.

Bonjour, mon élève! she says brightly as if entering the classroom of his life. And he answers *Bonjour, madame!* every bit as brightly; his eyes tear; his hands in their boxes pound emptily together; his head begins to ache as if an icicle has passed through it, harsh with grit. He cautiously sets his head in her lap while she tries various endearments, calling him her kangaroo, her lion, her harvest mouse, her mole, her cabbage, her trout. After refusing aspirin, he agrees to drink water, then removes the boxes from his hands, as if unpacking himself from something bigger.

Who shot him, and why, are questions he has already shelved along with the origin of the Milky Way and the nature of cruelty. Beyond him, these things affect the lives of others, not his own.

Come clean, she says. Aren't you glad it's over?

Only after dirtying myself with it.

It *is* over, you know. He's still in the jail, but he's of no importance to you.

Only as a memory, he says. While he's alive there's always hope. It would be after they cut him in two that I might feel I'd nothing left to live for. I hope they keep him forever where he is. Rotting. Even though he's not my man. It took some accepting, that. After all. He just happened to come along. A fur from any fox would have done. *I'll* always have headaches, *he'll* always be wondering if they're going to change the law and take him outside one rainy morning in a shirt without a collar while his mother waits at the gate unable to look, they always have mothers, and then they'll read the sentence aloud to him, as if he didn't know what he'd done, and fasten him in, although he's already frozen with fear. Five minutes from go to stop. I'd hold the basket if they asked. I'd trip the lever. I'd mop up afterward. I'd help to lead him in, shove the crowd away that wants to rip him limb from limb. It's amazing how tactless people get on such occasions.

Not to mention beforehand, she rebukes him. I thought we weren't going to hear any more about it.

Only when I weaken, he tells her. Which is every day.

Then you need help.

Oh, I'm human all right, he says. Help is my birthright.

No, Poussif, help is your undoing. You need help like a charging lion needs the wings of butterflies. What you need, old lad, is a cage. You're dangerous.

Only to me, he whispers. And those near and dear. I'm a weight on them. I admit it. I am far too much.

Only when you reduce it to a life for a life.

His for mine, you mean.

Mine for yours, my Old Testament duck. That's the swap that's taking place. Then ours for someone else's!

Like dressed-up lovers standing with their arms around

each other on an early-morning beach, after having danced themselves to a standstill, he in tux and she in gown, they hardly move in this pattern. It has been said before, more or less. It amounts to a catechism, as with the lovers making vows and merely pressing their lips, their fronts, together. The unsaid is everything. Only the unsaid is new. Sharli cannot get back the used-up time and Poussif cannot withdraw. Locked together as if on a badge, though not in combat, they have a heraldic dignity, wasting each other's time while Paris goes about its business, from one electrifying boredom to the next, Poussif thinking I will volunteer to sit in his cell as long as I live if they will only take him out and do it. Not that he was the one I really wanted, but to show that they are still capable of doing it to *any* of them.

Sharli is pregnant, but he thinks only of lives taken, and does not even include her own in them. Of a life to come, baby or afterlife, there is no talking. Her responsibility, this. Why not tell him? The wounded Rat Man fathered a child. What an amazing thing. A deciduous tree has made a pine cone. One of the walking dead has come to life again. All around them, lives waste and wither under the impact of terrorists, disease, auto accident, and earthquake, but they two have made a third. She will tell him under the glide path, she decides. Or not in Paris at all. Or France. It is not that he will become jealous. He will feel utterly replaced, victim of a one-man massacre.

Or is she underestimating him? Maybe he is made of more resilient stuff. She tries to reason it out between classes at school, trying to imagine his voice saying it.

If Poussif can live, against all odds.

Then why cannot another? Against other odds?

I am twice with child. I have twins. She hears his punctured-sounding voice and flinches. What shall Rat Man be next? What is he going to be? Jekyll or Hyde?

But he is Rat Man no more. He has mutated into something undreamed of. One day not long ago, as if the wound in his yawn had made him hospitable to blood, he crouched behind her as she tended the stove and kissed her behind between her legs just where his nose could feel the bulge of cotton. It was that time of the month, from before she was with her latest child.

I kiss your little pad, madame, he said with ravishing simplicity, and half an hour later was dragging a bloodstained string away from her loins with his teeth. He became a sort of pearl diver for days on end.

Poussif dives for muff, she said, again and again, caught up in her idea.

And comes up roses, he says, laughing red-mouthed. They kissed and decided that blood smells like rust.

When he touches and jiggles her, she heaves about in glorious attunement and says: You must have been a girl once upon a time. They had to half kill you to bring you to life. Yes, you *must* have been a girl.

Then, he says, in a frugal ecstasy marred by the faint whistle in his speech, think what I'd be like now if they'd got me through the brain.

That's quite enough. You've a lot of wasted time to make up for. Now: concentrate. On your sex life.

Was that only recently? No, she realizes, it has been three months since he was shot, and he has not budged from her apartment, the TV, her bed. He still expects to see his face on the TV screen, but it never appears, although the Boche's does in this or that newscast as the scandal edges forward in a tumult of shame.

Time has not so much gone by as dropped away.

One hundred days ago. It already smells like winter.

She struck a match and the wax aroma in the wood made him cry for boyhood fires lit furtively at the edges of fields, in the overgrown country lanes, against broken-down walls where they baked potatoes. Or tried to. They always came out hard.

She oven-bakes some in their jackets after school, but he

burns his hands on them. Too evocative by far, they cool off in the refrigerator, which is not much bigger than her television set.

> *Poussif* (she sings to him, improvising)
> *From the Château d'Yf,*
> *I use Ma Griffe.*
> *They call me Piaf.*

Who's that? Aha, she thinks, he's fooling. If he really didn't know, he'd say *who?* You only say *who's that?* when you're playing dumb. I've caught him off guard.

She sings it again, this time with a *They-call-me-Mimi* intonation at the end, which he somehow recognizes with an allusion: They say Rossini said everything he wanted to do in this life he could do in bed.

No, it wasn't Rossini, I mean who composed it, it was—

He does not want to know. He knows what Rossini said. That is enough to hold on to.

Sixteen

Now, as the weather gets colder, Rat Man's cheeks begin to twitch uncontrollably. Neuritis, says a tubby, bearded doctor with an effusive manner although the one-word diagnosis is laconic. An affair of the facial muscles, he adds. The muscles disturbed by the passage of the bullet. His heart—

I thought, says Sharli, it was only a flesh wound.

There are always the nerves, he says. Everything passing through disrupts the nerves. The heart, the bowels.

Rat Man senses the city bedding down for winter without him. Was he a nine-day wonder? Was he a wonder at all? He has not the heart to repeat his act or resume his walks. New-born as a homebody, he has begun to learn something about time, of which he thinks there are two kinds. That which passes unnoticed, and that which has an attractive shape. In the first you die, in the second you live.

Nonsense, Sharli scoffs: you do both in both.

You live, says Rat Man, only when you affect things, not the other way round. You never want to feel you're just a passenger, but that's what I feel just now. It's a short-term thing that has come to stay. It's almost enough to make you believe in the gods.

Then, she says, you've got something out of it all. Just think of that crazy old Nazi in that lousy jail. Now, *he's* the one who knows about time. He eats it three times a day. Does he get supper too?

Rat Man can hardly muster his old misplaced hatred. All he knows is that anyone pursuing something becomes that something to some extent. For a while he was the Boche, and now he is neither the Boche nor his former self. He feels transparent, open to the ragged wind of late November, almost like someone opened up on the operating table and left there, unfinished, in a draft from a broken window, with his mucous membranes exposed and drying.

Now then, she says, you're letting it begin. If you let it begin, then it's going to continue. And, if it continues, then you are going to have to live with it for the rest of your days, however many there are.

It begins and ends without any help from me, he tells her. It's time to go to Menton or Tahiti. We've used Paris up.

How could you? she murmurs. Paris is inexhaustible. You're just having a little sulk. You can no more exhaust Paris than you can empty the sea of fish.

No, he says, it's time. Time I was gone.

Using whose traveler's checks? I wonder.

I'll bum my way, he says valiantly, with a little doubtful smile. I wouldn't want to be a burden.

Then don't weigh so heavy, she says. I have a job even if you don't. I'm inventing the future.

I'm wondering, he answers, if there ever was a past. And if there was, if I was in it. I feel as if I've been sneaked in through a secret door. Like an illegal alien who can't remember where he came from.

Well, she tells him, I keep the records. If you're not sure, ask me, and I'll say. You don't have to remember, you just have to ask. Remember to ask and you can forget the rest. Why, you're shivering.

Oh, I will hardly die of it, he says buoyantly. Mind you, anything can lead to anything. Pinpricks lead to blood poisoning. A little tap on the elbow can give you cancer. It's been proved. You're almost afraid to walk about—you might inhale something, or bump into something, or get scratched. Maybe it's time they shot me into space. To store me up.

Poussif, she says with almost dainty candor, there are no Nazis in space. There are no Jews on Jupiter. It's mainly empty.

They haven't ballsed it up yet, he says. Wait. One day they'll shoot all the undesirables up there in big stainless-steel pumpkinlike things, which means that they'll eventually be in the majority. Then they will unfreeze themselves and set up the million-year Reich. The million–light-year Reich. He beams at so complex a conceit.

Why don't you read your newspapers more carefully, Poussif? A light-year is a unit of distance, not of time.

Not to me, he says. It sounds better the other way. Like something hopeless. Like how far can a day travel at the speed of light? I think about such things, and it's like climbing into the middle of a banana. Anyway, I can see myself being shipped out real soon. They will have to. My reputation's bad. I've made trouble in the streets. The police have my name. I was responsible for them picking up that little lame Spanish guy, the novelist, and all he was doing was watching Paris. He had nothing to do with me.

Very distinguished too, she coos. You intersected with somebody really well known. I'm amazed they arrested him. No, picked him up. He wouldn't shoot the likes of you. His mother was killed in one of Franco's air raids. *He'd* be on your side.

Not, he says wearily, if I was advertising a Nazi. And I was.

The trouble with you, she says, with a solemn wink, you don't understand how the literary mind works. They hang around looking for raw material. They don't care what you do so long as you do something they can turn into a best-seller.

But don't you think, *chérie,* he says, using an endearment for once and making her suddenly nervous, don't you think they would arrange to have a fellow shot through the chops just to have something different to write about? A painter needs a landscape. Your sculptor has to hew a chunk of marble. I don't see why your novelist of whatever nationality shouldn't cook up an incident in the streets just to give his imagination a kick. It *is* imagination they write those things with.

No, she says, fed up, they write them with the balls of their feet. In piddle places. With blindfolds on. And hot sandwiches pushed under the door by air hostesses from Afghanistan. Honest, Poussif, you'd better calm down. You've not only let it begin. You've built it into a roaring fire. I think you need a Sunday cuddle. Twice as long as a weekday one. Undo your shirt.

Not right now, he says. Haven't you ever felt neglected by an entire city?

She has had enough. On goes the TV and he leans to caress the static on the screen, daubing his initials in the faint veneer of dust. It is as close as he gets.

Over the next few days, however, he begins to prevail, insisting that his own fate outweighs hers. Silly billy, she calls him, trying to prepare three classes, one on Napoleon, one on Louis Pasteur, one on Matisse's chapel. She lives in a rich world full of beguiling corrugations. He dwindles, mainly on the rug of her apartment, eating only asparagus and bread. Deep in the banana, as he says. Sheathed in its peel. The doll's house sits unplayed with in the bedroom, with his few remaining props shoved untidily inside. The one picture remaining in his mind's eye, based on a newspaper photograph but outrageously deformed, comes and goes. Abject, hunched over a small cognac, with a thick rug over him, the Boche cradles his amputated head next to the one he still retains. In this way the Boche can see how bad he has been and what the consequences are. Such is Rat Man's impossible reward. The living and the dead come together in a ghastly huddle, and he almost feels a certain sympathy for the butcher from Bolivia. After all, they were once quite close. He impersonated the swine. He made him famous in the streets far from where the nation locked him up. The man's pain speaks to the pain in Rat Man, his impresario, and now, whispering his own nickname to himself, *Poussif, Poussif,* Rat Man puts both arms around his own head and hugs it, one hand atop a shoulder, the other in the armpit, and sits like that for half an hour, as if attuning the part of him still alive to the part of him long gone.

A pretty pose, she says, arriving red-cheeked and pert from the crisp outside air, not to mention hauling three days' groceries while with child. What's up?

He has no answer, but wonders vaguely if he resembles a python, a knot, or a saint in a stained-glass window.

Squeezing yourself again, she says. Well. I'm here now. You can relax.

But he can't, he wants to wind himself up tighter and tighter until he disappears. He has lost what he thinks miraculous when he finds it, or imagines it, in others: the gift of getting from minute to minute, hour to hour, as if all of that were not part of a life given you to be lived out. How he envies those maestros of in-between time. There must be several million of them in Paris alone. Just as many in Menton. No, fewer, but those in Menton might be better at it. His head begins to fail. His ability to compare dies out. He thinks, if he thinks coherently, in superlatives, out on a limb among the winners.

Muddle through, he whispers to her. Get by. Somehow cope. One day at a time. Just managing. I can't do any of that, like other folk. I want every day to be Christmas Day, see. Or Bastille Day. My head feels ready for magnificent things to happen, but there aren't any left. There are just the doldrums.

You sound like Louis the Fourteenth, she says. And all that. You want to eat cake every day. In this country they used to cut the heads off folk who thought like that.

No, he says. Asparagus will do me every time. I just want a bit of splendor, rained on or smeared with dog muck, I don't mind. Just a generous helping of something special.

Try me, she says. For a while there, you were coming back to life like a tornado. I had a man between the sheets. A lover. There was no satisfying you. Or me. Wasn't that special? Something that special can happen again. All you need is, that's right, a generous helping of protein. Turkey, eggs, beans, why God in heaven a lump of cheese would make you amorous. What about it? I haven't the time, but I'll make it. Where there's a will, my old snoot, there's a cry of mutual joy. Those who don't fill their days, their evenings at least, don't get them back, any more than those who do. It's a law of the living. I don't like to think of a double bed as a family mausoleum.

I'm beyond bed, he says. I need magic.

Seventeen

I'm as much magic as you're going to get, she says despondently, slicing him some cheese and tearing off a lump of bread. Apart from the cathode-ray tube in that little cabinet.

Do you think, he asks, that little novelist fellow is writing me up? If we found him, we could maybe read what he says.

I would think, she says, he's been watching millions besides you and me. Anyway, my champion of paralytics, he was on his way to Morocco when they ran him down. Eat up. He's had enough of you by now, I bet.

He's writing me up in Morocco, then.

Or just about anybody else. So, you like the cheese?

But I'd be mentioned. A few lines. Then, when I was gone, if I'm not gone already, people could point to the book in question and say: He lived, oh he lived all right. There's the proof. A certain Spaniard watched over him and set things down. He was there in Rat Man's heyday.

You really do want to be a famous old bugger, don't you? Or rather you want to be a famous bugger not quite so old as to have forgotten about yourself!

He fails to understand. She is sometimes too grammatical for him. If she talks in blurts, he follows. If she builds, as she truly knows how to, a sentence with fine distinctions bristling all through, he goes blank and eyes the ceiling, waiting for the angel of lucidity to descend. But nothing comes down on him save faint spots of whitewash dislodged by loud rock from above.

They kiss, but it's a token kiss only: a mouth truce. She is busy with schoolwork, he is busy with his unspent capacity for fame. He is willing, at this moment, to go to the guillotine himself, and he all of a sudden realizes how hard it is, these days, to get guillotined in France. He is living in the wrong country. Why, he thinks, even in such lovely spots as Bermuda and the Bahama Islands they hang folk still. It's only in the drab countries where they can't face capital punishment. France. England. It sort of adds to the general grayness. Whereas where the sun is shining, they don't mind at all. They can always cheer themselves up afterward by looking at the blue-green ocean, the pink sand, the bougainvillea. Why did I never think of that before? I would be the first to buy the excursion one-way special, first-class airfare all the way, a few days in a luxury hotel to get ready and calm down. Then the final event after you show your passport to prove who you are. He knows just how it would go.

Seat five-E, on the left, sir. The hanged, the hanged-to-be, is a little late arriving. By the time of the next one, we will be serving light refreshments. And there will be a properly printed program. Season tickets. Life membership. Suggestion box on the way out, sir. Anyone you think would make a nice ceremony, please nominate. A small gratuity for nominations that actually work out. Hot compresses? As on the airlines? Of course. And earphones, linked to the doctor's stethoscope. Polaroid pictures permitted, of course. Gift shop in a year or so.

I wouldn't mind, he thinks. I'd go through with it if they would. It might take a bit of getting used to, for some not from among the hanging crowd, but everything takes time. They'd understand. If you changed your mind, they wouldn't hold you to it, but they'd charge you extra for the return trip. And that would cost more than the usual excursion fare. All the same, you could leave it open. Is that what they call an open-jaw ticket?

He asks her. She shows him her checkbook. Not that he is an expensive house guest; it's just that his presence has made tiny inroads. She has to keep the place hotter and brighter. He burns light at night, pottering about while she sleeps. Asparagus is pricey.

Oh, he says in a huff, I'm a burden.

She reminds him she is pregnant. Asleep when she gets up, he has never seen the morning sickness, but he likes the way she seems to have bloomed and ripened, even though sexually he is far from busy. He loves her, now, with a painter's eye. Rubens. He loved fatness. He eyes her breasts, waist, and loins, he nods and murmurs: *Something nice at every level.* I wish I was more of a fucker. If you paint, you don't have to fuck half as much, but if you don't paint, well, it gets past joking about. Just look at her. The world is spoiling me rotten these days. If I could bear smoke, I'd be a smoker. Of imported Camels. And I'd tip the ash into the cuffs of my pants whenever there was no ashtray. All my pants have cuffs.

Cherub, she calls him, then flower, dunce, chaffinch, rabbit, *chéri,* cauliflower, Father Time, Nazi hunter, tiger, lollipop, duffer, Your Highness, granddad, Poussif *père,* but it is all the same to him. He goes about his chores, sharpening her pencils over a garbage bag and meticulously dusting the little German sharpener afterward, or boiling the kettle as if it were a feat that few accomplish (he holds it all the time as if it might fall away from the flaming gas). Daily he wipes the TV screen, thrilled when the hairs on his wrist lift in the static charge. As he sees it, he is busy, leading a full life, while she, invisibly growing their child and heir within her trunk, comes and goes with gently deteriorating good humor. The nightmare she envisions is trying to get Poussif to take her to the hospital in an emergency; first he will sharpen her pencils, boil the kettle, wipe the screen, heedless of her pain. Maybe it is me he really wants to execute, she thinks. He sees life as a process in which there are no human preferences. He'll kill us all one day without so much as noticing.

Then she forgives him, makes allowances for the trauma of his childhood, the fiasco of his manhood, the anticlimax of his recent obsession.

When a roach shows up in the bathroom, she calls him in, and he tries to steer it onto a piece of toilet tissue he sets down, so as not to stain the floor. But the roach goes everywhere else until, in desperation, he squashes it on the speckled linoleum. Now he scrubs and sprays, wipes and dusts, eliminating not only every last vestige of roach but also the sheen on the floor. After squirting after-bath cologne where the stain used to be, he encases the remains and the used tissue in a plastic sandwich bag, then this in another, and then that in yet another, saying he will go somewhere to burn it all.

You can't burn plastic, she says, it makes a poison gas.

Never mind, he says jauntily, I'm one of the roaches of history. There are other ways. Twenty minutes later, he has folded a rather handsome paper airplane from a sheet of stiff drawing paper and taped the little bundle across the top of the wings. One test flight, diagonally across the living room, and he is ready. In comes the gust as he launches through the streetside window, nodding at how well it flies. It almost nose-dives, but the weight gives it momentum, the near-dive gives it lift, and it gracefully skims the face of someone in uniform, maybe that of the French Foreign Legion, who swats it aside without losing step. The roach has crashed.

A big effort, she tells him. There was hardly need. Are you going to fly the garbage out the window from now on?

He refuses to tell, but wants to discuss names for the child who will be born late next summer. No Alphonse, he insists, and no Etienne.

It may not be a boy. There are two sexes.

We will meet that when we come to it, he says. How about Charles? As in Chelsea.

Very sweet, she says. I wouldn't mind. But already he is ushering her into the bathroom again, pointing to a fleck of scab, a tiny thing, he has brushed or combed from his head into the washbasin. It has leaked into a small blob of water which is now palest carmine. He sees a recent piece of himself in the act of dissolving. I could become a donor, he says. Blood, anyway. I don't know about the other thing.

Suppressing her laugh, she informs him that Poussif as a sperm donor would be like . . . no, she cannot say it. She thinks it. He waits. Still she says nothing. Maybe she is going to stroke his chest, as sometimes at the airport when he gets excited.

However little of it there is, he blusters, it seems to work. How many spoonfuls, anyway, would it take to make a regiment? It's the other way round. There aren't enough women to accommodate it. Meager as the supply might be. They both smile, then gently laugh, proud parents-to-be. A visitation from the future is between them, comfy as a small cushion.

He says so, but she corrects him: Not that big, yet. You'll see. We'll need a bigger bed.

Damn and blast, he says, I wish we'd kept that pram. What are we going to wheel it about in? Not *it.* Him or her. I suppose. We don't make neuters here.

We have a car, she reminds him. We'll drive to all kinds of places. Hot and cold. Hot, anyway. Just wait. Why, even that doll's house of yours will come in handy. I foresee a proud papa having a good play.

That's right, he says, and he at once forgets the whole thing, musing again on becoming a donor. I'd need new feet, he says absently. Shoes, I mean. Before we went anywhere. Now he knows why his pants are cuffed. He likes to look down into something: a cleft of lint. His cuffs gape, always, but she isn't interested in cuffs, although she sees the connection. Sharli is intent on shoes.

It's easy, she says. You just go and buy them.

They would see my heels. They might refuse.

Oh no, she says cautiously, they'll sell to anybody who has money or credit. You don't even have to have feet. It's a free society on the outside. Honestly. Anyway, your heels are much better. You don't walk. How can you have calluses anymore? Show me. He has healed up, his heels feel smooth and supple, scarred of course, but no longer like weathered and split teak.

While we're about it, she tells him, we can get you a whole new outfit. You can smoke a pipe. Carry a cane. In the winter, there are overshoes for any size. Don't worry. Things are there for folk to use. It says so in the sociology books my kids take home to read. Nothing's there to hurt you. What a funny society it would be that refused to manufacture shoes, or sell them, just to get people all upset. Things don't work that way. Take it from me, Poussif. Life is good. It caters to the living, not the damned, the dead.

He smiles his war-is-over smile. He has been spoken to from Antares. He almost takes what she says on trust, but a piece of his mind still awaits the first calamity in the pattern.

And, she says heavily, I don't want you donating anything I could use. The money's nothing, the donation is all. Donate to me. I'm off the pill of course. I'm kind of invulnerable now.

He understands. What, he asks in his discombobulated fashion, is the male equivalent of a woman with child?

There isn't one. There can't be one. He has to identify with the woman.

What if the man went sterile for the same period? Poussif seems to have much more advanced ideas than usual. Then, he resumes, the man wouldn't be able to get any other woman with child. Even if he tried.

She marvels at his dream of promiscuity: the Man in the Iron Mask advertising shaving foam. This is the man who, at weekends, has to be coaxed into waking up. Sleep fits him only for further sleep. The more he has, the more he needs. It was not always so, when he tramped the streets. What has undone him, she tells him, is the soft suburban life, the pampering, the bread-and-asparagus ease, the murmuring rainbow screen in the small apartment. Why, he no longer fusses with the miniature patio.

I do in summer, he says. Never now.

What's the difference? The leaves . . . She sighs.

I like to see them, he says. The ground looks nearer.

How can you see the ground through the leaves?

The leaves *are* the ground. It's like walking on foam. Like a dry surf. Very soothing. What's left of them I'll tidy up in the spring, before the birth.

If we're still in Paris.

I'd come back, he promises, and do the patio. I'd make it neat before I left, I'd like to think of that, wherever else I was. The leaves will keep. Take it from an old streetwalker like me. Nobody needs them. Ever.

She marvels at the concealed originality of ordinary beings. Rat Man has depths, but he has shallows too. He doesn't have to reveal all of himself, surely; the quickest way of becoming a bore is to tell everything. Instead of countering him, or even taking him seriously, she tends a little slum of rancid fruit in the refrigerator, surprised at herself—she is acting as if they are both going away somewhere for—well, what would it be? A Christmas vacation? How would I manage that? she wonders. I get sleepier and sleepier with each day.

I'll soon be a swollen zombie. Yet everything that counts gets done by busy people. Those with leisure achieve nothing at all. What shall I do with Poussif? When he was roaming the streets, he was one thing; he could more or less be relied upon. But now, having lived out his delusion, and having been shot for his pains, he's not as easy to manage. Maybe the strain of living sober will drive him to death by drink. He's bound to have a future of some sort, for which I am going to be responsible. Cut him adrift? Would he last a week, a day, or just possibly for year after year? Is he one of those creaking gates you hear about? Vulnerable as a newborn baby, but tough as an old goat who's drunk nothing but water and inherits hardy genes.

She cannot fathom him, thinking the perpetual child never grows up and therefore never dies, but waits to be hosed down in the barn by Madame R. Yet those who outlast the random hammerblows of war succumb to a pinprick, a common cold, like Emile Zola dying of the fumes from a stove. There is no way in which she can foretell his fate. She can no more abandon him than she can cut his throat. Yet a nuisance he is bound to be. He's been one all along, in fact. But, with a baby on the premises, demanding everything of her, what is Rat Man going to do? Is he going to have an entire new career based not on revenge but jealousy? The thought sickens her, so she turns to busywork, removing the thick rubber band from a wad of index cards on which, over the years, she has written down chores to be done sooner or later. Usually, she takes out one at random and does the work prescribed, but now she shuffles them all on the table, idly noting this or that item, and in the end doing none of them.

Get out your nasties, she calls, meaning his dirty laundry, of which there is little. He owns the minimum and wears it all, or at least as much of it as he can. He will often accost her in two shirts with, hidden, a double set of underwear. This is why nothing he wears is ever really clean. Now he enters from the kitchen, murmuring something about touching the private area of the body, but unable to finish the thought.

Everything off, she instructs him. You can sit naked until I come back. Use a blanket. He does, but with a scowl, and then offers to do the laundry for her without meaning it.

You'd drown yourself, she says, wondering if she could become an exchange teacher with someone in the South who wanted to come to Paris, where winter is exciting only to those who live their lives elsewhere. A stopped-up sink convinces her. The water from the last washing of the dishes floats in front of her, coated with a ragged scum of grease and bubbles. Rat Man offers, but she dreads the flood, the wounds he will inflict on the plastic pipe beneath, the stainless steel of the sink itself. Off she goes, weary and aching to vomit, with the candy-striped laundry bag over her shoulder, Rat Man in his blanket, with the powders and the bleach. If he comes with her, he sits in the car, claiming he cannot breathe in the laundromat; so, usually, she sends him back to the apartment, vainly mentioning the patio, but afraid to mention the sink.

She need not have worried. Into the kitchen he comes, gives a wincing scowl at the rubber gloves laid flat, and begins scooping water from the sink with a big saucepan, marching to the bathroom to empty it into the toilet. This done, he runs hot water into the sink until it reaches the scum line of before, and sits down to watch TV. He has made his gesture, not so much like someone who reconstructs the lives of the victims from the wreckage of a plane as one who divines the crash in all its detail from the planeload of people. Next time he empties the sink, the water will still be clean.

More water, he murmurs, watching a travelogue about the Riviera, marking a pencil-sharp nipple as the taut cone of a breast lolls away from its cup, marveling as woman after woman marches past the judges of a beauty contest in swimsuits that cover their pubic areas with a strip of fabric no wider than a scabbard. Slit skirts have had the same effect on him, reminding him to be sexual, lost in a voluptuous tedium of his own, listening to reason if he can, but somehow untuned. Out of it. Out of himself. Muddled physically, as inclined not to perform as to do so. Not the accidental man, or the man without qualities, or the sloth-bound man, but the man undistributed, most of him in a storage so cold he cannot reach it even with his mind. Yet he notices how the idiom of the TV commercials is more complicated than that of the rock songs he hears but fails to understand. Of course, he thinks, *they* want to sell you something; the others are just howling about something that remains their own.

At the bathroom mirror he stares at the faint graphite rings under his eyes, clue to a peptic ulcer he believes will not have the gall to challenge him or try to steal the game from the heart that quite airily dances about in his chest even when he is calm as can be. Much of him, he decides, has a life of its own, a destiny having little to do with him. Which is fine. So much of us is borrowed, he thinks; you can't ask all of it to behave well, as if you'd gone out and bought it at a bicycle store or a pharmacy. What was it she'd said as one day they had slid haunch to haunch along the polished bench at the counter in an American-style coffee shop?

At my age I shouldn't be having a baby at all. Anybody's. I'm not that old but I'm getting too old for that. I'll have it all the same. I spend my working weeks with other people's kids. At least, if I have one of my own, it'll age alongside me, so to speak, whereas with the others they stay the same age every year while you keep getting on a bit.

So: she is having it for her, not him. Just as well. Should he get out of her life, then, and leave her to it? No, he cannot bear to think of it, useless as he is. So, if he stays, what must he learn to do? What on earth will this child be like? Will it change their lives once and for all? He wishes he were in America. Anywhere far away. Unobligated to the life process, he does not wish to be involved with people, but with phantoms only, and Sharli is far too real. Even the Spaniard has faded away, to write about somebody else, not Rat Man or Poulsifer. Who else will proclaim him now?

When she returns with the laundry, he warms his face in the burned-smelling towels and fails to notice the decision in her face. Two weeks later, though, after she has contracted an exchange for the entire year, December to December, he realizes the full scope of her will to live. Behind them the kitchen sink is still more or less clogged, but they drive south in an almost awestruck silence, dreaming of warmth and a wet rather than a snowy winter. All the way down, it rains persuasively, but lets up after Grenoble, and soon they are close to Nice. He does not even notice that, as they go through Lyon, not that far behind them, they have come within striking distance of the butcher from Bolivia, the sadist from Peru. In any event it would have been enough for Rat Man to think, simply, this excursion to the sun will be denied him for ever and ever. They arrive exhausted, but to an average sun, and Sharli has three days' grace before going off to teach merely in order to end the term. They settle in, wearing much the same clothes as in Paris, and they stare greedily at the sea as if it holds something, deep down, it is going to yield up to them.

Not exactly bemused, but not quite attentive either, Rat Man branches out, doing his best not to trade on his up-North reputation. One day soon, perhaps, there will be a Rat Man moving along the Boulevard des Anglais, built by workers from the orange groves when the crop of 1822 failed. No wonder, he thinks, Nice is called Nice because the Greeks called it *Nike,* meaning "victory." The beach is rocky, but the bathhouses provide mattresses for a small fee. This, he knows, is a place that will do. And so will he, in it. Once more a phantom engrosses him, at least until the baby comes. But this is a phantom of someone else's devising: a Trevi fountain in the South of France. One night in ten he sleeps, but on the other nine he sweeps the drained fountain with his broom and gets to keep the coins flung in. The wishes fondly willed that graced the coins have long since come true, or not, but in a sense they all are his. One day soon, once we have the baby and enough, he tells those he talks to in the nights, we'll aim a little higher and move on to Rome.

But they do not. Rome is far away, and Poussif realizes how long a baby takes to form. Yes, it's the brain that slows things up. Except for that, we'd slither out of our mommas in a brace of weeks. It's getting the brain big enough to be smart enough later to go bonkers that takes forever.

Sucking an orange in the midday sun, he half grins the satisfaction of one who has just gone through a complex scientific proof. Now, on juiced fingers, he tallies her symptoms, as weird to him as tropical fish laid wriggling on a wedge of toast.

Take the morning sickness that also comes by night. Why not call it the sickness of before and after? In spite of it, she goes off to teach with a look of heroic containment that makes him feel unwanted and scared. Then the listlessness. She hardly moves, except when forcing herself to go out: curled up on the threadbare couch, not asleep but marooned, a lioness pausing in the heat, fattening from within, with a new sheen to her arms and face as her skin tightens.

The other side of this coin, he reminds himself, is that she cannot get comfortable in bed. She heaves, writhes, tosses, she who has always slept on her front. And, she tells him with the forlorn gravity of a martyr, she itches, she tingles, with excess blood. Hyper-something, she says.

The extra salts, he says knowingly, and recommends hot-water douches, as if he knew.

Almost accustomed to being butted awake, or kept by commotion from the last few seconds of drifting off, he suggests the couch, then goes to it himself, unable to figure out why, on her days off school, she can sleep all through the day in seeming comfort, but can't rest easy at night. Because, he decides, the day sleep kills the nighttime one. Wrong: after a harsh full day at school, she comes home exhausted but also in an endless fidget. If, he thinks, afternoon came again after sunset, and then again at midnight, she'd still be unable to settle. Afterdusk, he'd call the one. The other would be something else.

He gives up. The key to it all is his being beside her in bed. Sneaking to the bedroom door, he listens hard, but she seems to be sleeping soundly. Some mornings he has to rouse her, she does not hear the alarm, or anything else.

Now she seems a beef, a whale. No, not so lumpish. She has become a luminous bulge, a swaying waddler with chubby cheeks, her expression one of painful cheeriness, aching to tell him some unspeakable good news, but always holding back at the last moment. He studies her face and wonders at its cascade of moods, from aloof appraisal to unsettled tenderness, from satisfaction to a look of astute tolerance never before seen except on the face of his mother's fox fur.

Eighteen

Ranging back and forth among words available to him, he tries to pin down what's different, and what survives of the old Sharli. Her moods vary so fast. He might as well attempt to state the mood of the iris of an eye. She seems both away on loan to another order of beings and overly present: a near, dear, faraway other who looks through him into some crystal ball of bliss.

Out of it, he whispers. Who'd dare touch her? She'd bruise. Or acid would squirt out of her. You'd have to get permission from the Salvation Army. Wear mittens made of dandelion fluff. Hands off, Rat Man, my boy, there's dirty work at the crossroads every night, at least at hers. I'd no more put a hand near there than I'd, well, I don't rightly know. It's all my fault, but I myself have no pregnancy symptoms. None. That's the funny, lonely side of it. Maybe if there were something there for me, something welcoming, I'd risk it. She is a vessel, not like a ship with barnacles, but a jug, within it cut dahlias planted in vinegar.

A taboo, word too close to tobacco to be taken seriously, has nonetheless come home to him. He tries to spell it out, but only blunders from puzzle to puzzle, in the end having to settle for her being mysteriously apart for reasons unknown. Known only to kangaroos. She does not lay eggs. If she did, he'd love to be the broody hen and sit them out. Having no symptoms at all save feeling out of it, he feels used up in one go. What he did has no future within him. I am a spout, he tells the peel cup of his orange. A kettle. A blowgun. A water pistol. It has gone away from me into her tripes, never to be seen again, cooked until done. Oh, I could take an interest, as they say, but only at a distance, with hands off. One little gob of syrup and the whole system says thanks, mate, and turns its back.

Yet now and then couvade gets him nearer her. Thinking he too should throw up, he knows he is going to, shoves a finger down his throat, but merely hawks a series of dry heaves.

Have you got something stuck? She asks this when he tries it only within arm's reach. Have *you?* he croaks.

He pretends to purr and doze, a full lion on the Serengeti, yawning and lazily swatting flies with a paw. But sleep he cannot, nor enter her brand of thick oblivion, as if she has curdled and gone solid, each part of her weighing the others down farther and farther until she is so gravid—he finds the word at last—she slowly bores a hole through the cushions on her way to the core of the earth, where all her trouble begins. Once there, she could not possibly fall away to Australia; the core would not allow it.

Young cells, he mumbles as he tosses the orange peel into his own fountain, I never had none of those. I'm ungrammatical. Mine were secondhand, hand-me-downs from warped bullfrogs and broken crocuses. Like stars with blunted points. They refused to work together. Now look at me, Rat Man turned coin collector. At only half rat power these days, with a son or girl in the offing. An heir in the oven. Where the hell *is* the offing? I am very much like your average Arctic explorer, out in the drifts and crevasses with all dogs eaten, and only a candle to burn or to eat between me and the polar dark.

Rat Man, he commands himself out there in the sunshine, buck up. A night worker should be fast asleep.

Be brave. Up to scratch. Come into your own.

Come to. Come into your hand.

Be like other men. He laughs tartly, recalling a radio program (he clocked it) in which the explanation of an opera took longer than the opera itself. They do like to talk about their music, don't they? Once upon a time I talked about mine, before my eclipse. Bass-baritone of the boulevards.

He feels dependently cut off as if Sharli has gone back into the universe and left him on the doorstep. With, alongside him, not so much as an empty bottle for him to fill in case baby Rat Man needs a boost, needs topping off, a better batch of brain cells, or cells of any stamp.

It doesn't work like that, you soft Aladdin; she's tight as a walnut, that's the way she is. You could no more slip a tiddler past her own private St. Peter than you could enter the St. Joseph jail. Why is everything out of reach? It's when what's rightly reachable goes beyond you that you get peevish. Heartsick. A word comes, he barely comprehends it, but it evokes a whole range of verbs, a whole class called deponent, which he remembers as verbs that lie down and die, like dogs that have eaten rotten offal. Yes, he decides, I'm deponent. That's me. It being his water, his fountain, he slides his feet, knees, thighs, waist, chest, and face right into it and hopes to drown.

Those who see him look away, permissive and kind. He's hot, he'll soon be cool. Down in the shallows, with coins faintly imprinting his buttocks, he hears, he identifies, an Airbus going over, and up he cranks himself, blinking water, to spot the plane before it becomes a mere wisp. Airbus it is, he'd know it anywhere, even while giving up the ghost in the Arctic. He yearns for the end of the runway, where big wings waft the tiny open car up after them, aluminum tugging tin.

Yet his thoughts are not aerial. If a child of our time becomes the man of tomorrow, he argues after sneezing, what am I? Not even yesterday's child. What am I now? Do I grow from being no child into no adult, and from that into an unknown ghost? That is, a ghost who is the ghost of nobody. A ghost's ghost? No, yesterday's ghost turns into tomorrow's nobody. I have discovered philosophy at last. I use words about what does not exist.

How fast he is drying off, although not out. Having cooled his heels, the rest of him, he considers a whole new way of life. Dunk and dry, dunk and dry, until he shrinks enough to be in a womb or a tobacco pouch. Safe as houses. Bitter, he resolves to have his emissions checked, as if he were a car. He would like to splash the baby's head, just once, in a wash of fellow feeling. Oh, more tenderly than that. *Bonjour, mon petit, ma petite.* Do you hear the thump of Sharli's heart? What language do you talk in there?

Nineteen

Having invented philosophy, he feels free to think anything, and never mind the decent, fatherly view of the little stranger in her midst. He wants back something of his own, and he doesn't want to have to wait for it. He is being burned alive at the stake near the North Pole. He is all kinds of shivers, and longs for a clime where the air is clear, the sky so high and dry, the warmth so rigid, that you live two days in one. Arizona or Mexico. Peru. Bolivia. Those kinds of places. Is that what the Spanish novelist writes about, he too a misfit among parents, puritans, and policemen? When will he start page one? If ever.

Back to the sun, Poussif sees a motley throng gazing past and through him, his azure dungarees to them no more than a scab of Menton blue. To them he is not, by day or night.

He is not even a nonentity. He has not figured in their century as Rat Man did in Paris, or the Boche worldwide. He sneezes again, clears his throat. Barks, coughs, goes from a yelp to a squeak, but no one leaps across the intervening two meters to give him the kiss of life. Or the fireman's lift. Or a quick clasp below his rib cage to eject a choking morsel from his throat.

This, he decides, must be how it is in the electric chair. Or under the blade. Friendless throng with no eyes. So near, so far. So native, so foreign. An unfaked hiccup seizes him, followed by dozens more, and he clucks away to ask for a spoonful of sugar. Each hiccup, he knows, is a little death. Each time his penis pops too. So is each death a hiccup or a pop? Death, he decides, fumbling a bit, is the only unthinkable thing you can have occasional thoughts about without doing any damage. No, he remembers black magic, the evil eye, those who think themselves to death in or out of the Sorbonne. There is one thing about death, though; it ends the worry about other deaths. Beheaded, you no longer dread being hanged. Hanged, you no longer shrink from the blade. In the old days, though, they tried to do everything to you before you kicked the bucket, almost all at once. Hanged, disemboweled, beheaded, in that order. The Chinese went in for it. He once saw a photograph of a priest subjected to the ritual of a thousand cuts, after which—Poussif shakes his head. What he keeps trying to tell himself is that you have to put up with one death only and that's your lot. Almost a relief, at the end, isn't it, to know the heart isn't going to do to you what the cancer did, and vice versa. Or the bullet the hangman. We are linked to life, he decides, like the old folks to their morsel. They bring it to their mouth, then put it down, and it trails a string of spit after it all the way, which stays until they try again, and then it breaks or the string becomes double, and soon there is a little silver cat's cradle between them and it. If such things weren't meant to be, they wouldn't happen. Or would they? His hiccups have gone. He has found the cure: to get rid of something, think about something worse. What, then, is worse than death? Could he but think of that, he would be sitting pretty. If walking on eggs, he tells himself, do not hop.

Another audience sees him now, greeting acquaintances with his forefinger set against his jugular; now and then seeming to wrestle a supermarket cart as it cants this way or that across an aisle; learning to be obsequious without getting effusive; saving up his faint praise for something that never comes. He stomps on crickets in the shower stall, refusing to spray, and even, on one occasion, gets fastidious, trying to clean his ears with cotton swabs from Sharli's bathroom cabinet.

My ears are too small, he complains.

Duffer, she scolds. These are for makeup, not for ears at all. They're twice the normal size. Now, have you gone and done your ears an injury? Ruptured the drum? I suppose not. The devil looks after his own. Luck, like respect, is what you have to have in order to get it.

Meanwhile, in another city, the guessed-at Spanish novelist, not lame at all (Rat Man grafted that on to him), types a first sentence that runs *Even as the executioner squeezed the trigger, Rat Man, with a rope around his neck and his hands tied behind his back, saw as he kneeled the inscription on his own ready-made grave, and felt the selfish, sterile pleasure of martyrdom,* for some reason italicizing from the outset. He sits back, scowls, spins the sheet from the machine and sets it aside, to be pondered or torn. Rat Man's fame hangs in the balance. Now the novelist, still sitting at the typewriter, begins to dream about Lawrence of Arabia, Damascus, Baghdad, and Istanbul, Ottoman locomotives and the stiff bristling hairs of his (Lawrence's) handlebar mustache. The stronger image wins, and Rat Man can go about his business unmeddled with, at least in Spanish prose. The skeptical sideways glance of the face below the close-cropped quiff will touch on him no longer, although the novelist himself, in olive trench coat and beige scarf, almost looks like the Rat Man of Barcelona, too well known to skulk, however, unless he goes to London or Oxford, trailing Lawrence of Arabia, a richer myth by far than any Man of Rats.

Twice a day Rat Man dunks himself, and then he tries it at night. Invisible, he attracts notice only at the clinic when, dressed in his suit, he escorts Sharli through whiplash spring-loaded doors, and the clinicians have the same response as always: What's the matter with *him?*

They see his untanned scars, an inoculation blotch in either cheek, glossy salmon color etched with darker dots, almost like two navels in his face. Again they ask, half hypnotized.

Not *him,* he's in the pink. Sharli flaps her hands toward herself. It's me, as usual. Don't you people remember anybody?

But they go on seeing and appraising this poleaxed, punctured-looking ogre with the disheveled face, who seems unable to breathe or speak, terrified they are going to anesthetize him there and then, and operate just to see what makes him tick. Walk this way, m'sieu.

Not today, he blurts. Women and children first.

At last she goes in to the nurse, and Poussif, devastated to be alone in the reception room, finds an empty chair in a cubicle, then screens himself off. Someone in a paper shift returns and finds him there, sizzling his spit behind tight lips: an incarnation of the spirit of radiology. Ejected and yelled at, he offers to donate his body to science, but says nothing at all. The offer is a gesture. He prays, a domino prayer in which each word takes the next adrift: Our, no one's, parent, morning sickness. Not what he meant to pray at all.

You look anemic, someone says.

Oh yes. He likes to satisfy.

You're flaking. Too much sun. You should be careful.

All the time, he answers eagerly. And palpitations too.

Did you ever cough up blood? Are you ever short of—

Once I did, he says. A lot. It was a bullet.

You coughed up a bullet?

They examine his teeth, dismiss him as a liar with possible skin cancer and poor blood, and are just ushering him out the door when Sharli reappears wet-eyed. Not him, me, she hisses.

Always you, he tells her in the car. They were just beginning to take an interest in me, for all kinds of things. I'm an interesting case. I could stand quite still, stark naked, in some lecture hall, while they went on about all the things that ail me. I'd be the center of attention. I'd be *him.* The man. The one. Somebody central.

Look, my old sludge pump, she chides, you're not Rat Man anymore. You have had your cameras. What you are going to be is all cut out for you. It's work, yes, but it's a joy to come. It'll be the making of you.

But he does not want the making of him to start. I'm far too deponent already, he smiles, for that. A person of active meaning, but passive form.

Quite the word man, she quips. You've been reading again. Good old flower. The rest of the world turns its back on the book and you discover language at last. Jesus sawing up his deathbed.

I read for France, he explains. As others run or jump.

France needs you. Let's go home. They do, but only after shopping en route; Poussif clasps two packages of frozens against his chest to calm his heart. Or halt it.

Where are you now? In his mind, she means. He does not answer, but he knows he is finally cold.

You'll have to eat them if you thaw them out.

The heat of where *they* are, he says morosely, would not melt a chocolate drop. Honest. Those doctors in there, they might have wanted to pump me full of formaldehyde, and then lower me into a big glass jar with a label that says *Rat Man,* and then, in parentheses, *Paris.* Like that *Australop—*

She completes the word. How exotic it sounds.

Poussif Pithecus, he muses. That *would* be me. It has a musical sound. Clean as pumice. Good as gold. I'm quite warming to the idea of becoming a specimen.

Sometimes, after this much talk, they do not speak for hours, but linger in conjectural togetherness. Poussif smolders away at the Pole of his choice while she waits for the baby to kick. They do minor things with pliers, scissors, glue, and sticky tape. He fixes a knob that has fallen off the stove. She remounts and rearranges pictures in her photo album.

No one comes to see them. They have come here to be here, but not to be anyone for anyone here. As far as privacy goes, they have achieved it with paralyzing grandeur. And now, before she goes completely out of sight, he would like to leave, he thinks, yet as incapable of flight as an emu, as incapable of moving away as a tree. But he means to emigrate domestically, to have a home away from home, intact within his head, complete with fire irons, rugs, and a chiming clock from Switzerland. Those who cannot go from home, they home in on as distant a glow as the galaxies provide.

What his head provides, all of a sudden, as he waits the baby out, is an old shabby quarter in which globe-shaped lamps light up at dusk, and, because it is warm there, amputees in wheelchairs cruise about to walk their dogs. The women cut down the bushes and take them indoors for safekeeping. His ideal comes to life, of a merely token relationship with her, as with civilization, so that the most intimate, crucial bond he has is with the weather, with food, with the body's internal seasons from hiccup to yawn, from headache to waking, and never being obliged to go anywhere at all. Out if bright, back to sleep if dull.

Plus much. He knows it will fill out the more he ponders it. With no help from Sharli, the police, television cameras, Alphonse, tracker dogs, Spanish novelists, or assassins who shoot at the face. Or the Klaus Barbies of the world. He gasps as the name of the wrong man leaks into and from mind's mouth into mind's ear. He no longer cares to know the correct identity of the man who razed his boyhood village. Barbie will do, as just about any old age will serve to lead you up to death. No risk of disappointment there. He says the name aloud. I knew it all along. It doesn't hurt, it can't, it won't.

Twenty

When she goes into labor, it is Poussif's event as much as hers; his insides churn. A soccer ball heaves through his urethra. He dithers, almost spasms; she is going to be torn apart before his eyes.

This is Sunday, she reminds herself, so thank you to the patron saint of childbearing. But who will be there? Someone is always there. Is it May or June? So hot. Because it is Sunday, though, she is at Poussif's mercy and not in the capable hands of the ironic school principal, who views pregnancy as yet another form of cancer, whereas, to Poussif, as far as she can tell, it resembles a cosmic catastrophe forced into human scale: deformity leading to explosion, with somewhere toward the end strops and ribbons of innards floating dead in orbit around a red crater. She has pieced this together from his babble about jam and phosphorus, curd and sponge, seaweed and slimy fins. When he talks in his sleep he is more coherent than by day, when, to use his own word against him, as she does, he is too deponent to say anything at all. Active meaning, passive form, as he says.

All the same, he insists on phoning for the taxi, even as she wonders why he is so vague about his own birthday, in different years locating it in July, January, May. She has looked it up: April 2, and she wrote it down for him, and stuck to it with an airplane birthday card each year. He just, she decides, decided long ago. He doesn't want to be tied down. The cab will be there in fifteen minutes. It is. They go, Poussif carrying her bag of emergency supplies, into which, weeks ago, he popped a torn-out page of *Paris-Match,* showing him with his pram. He has folded it once, then once again. It will be his way of watching over her, invisibly folded in upon himself.

Could she have driven? Yes, but awkwardly confined. In spite of everything she begins to giggle; she has just thought of Poussif as a driver, which is like giving a Hottentot a typewriter, or a device to warn of police radar guns on the highways. She pursues the game to distract herself during the drive. Poussif driving is like awarding a giraffe a drip-dry shirt. Seating a sloth at the controls of a jumbo jet. The exact analogy refuses to come, and she decides it wasn't meant to. For its weird combination of the hopeless, the uncouth, and the unmechanical, Poussif in the driver's seat has no equivalent, in bestiary, heraldry, or demonology. Was he ever even born? Of course, but maybe he accreted, during the time on earth of the blue-green algae, assembling unknown and unknowingly like a plague, then in cold storage for countless years until started off again by some rare alignment of the sun, earth, and moon. That he could have been the pride and joy of music-loving bourgeois parents is preposterous.

The hospital comes into view as another ghastly thought, that of Poussif as midwife, erupts in her befuddled head. Oh no, not he, with carpenter's saw held aloft, an oil can by him on the floor, and rope galore to tie her down, not to mention the ancient baby carriage reeking of dead urine awaiting her last push, the first ride, the pulp-soft occupant.

She feels ashamed. He just happens to be among those, she concludes, who have no idea how to handle themselves, even during masturbation. Feckless, all thumbs, out of touch, beyond the pale, archaic and daffy all at once, but evil? No. Not a bad man, just a poor sample. A free gift. A warning of what a man becomes who lives without tradition, a code, a home.

She does not believe it, but at the top of the steps on which Nazis not long ago strutted and preened, a nurse, no an orderly, comes out, looks her in the eye and nods, then asks what is wrong with him. See how he gulps for breath—

Furious and in pain, she snaps: Can't you see? He's ready to pop. He's giving birth. You can see his contractions from streets away. She almost faints, but Poussif, laughing even as he trembles along his length, drapes an arm about her and seems to lift her up from invisible water.

Now all goes according to plan, and Poussif decides to wait although they tell him it might be half a day before the birth. He feels as if he is awaiting the onset of World War Ten, or the day the planet catches fire. Never has he felt less ready, more stranded. He who cannot run his own life needs no passengers. Is that an aphorism or a comment on him in particular? He begins to tear pages from the tattered magazines lying around, then soaks them in the men's room until he has a lump of papier-mâché the size of a sparrow, which he then begins to fashion into something, watched and quizzed by half a dozen of the anxious. A frog, he says uneasily. They see no frog. A rabbit, then. No rabbit seen. A thrush. Fresh from the Arabian palace of shape.

You, says a tense-looking mechanic in coveralls, seem not to be any good at that, m'sieu. It takes a certain gift.

No, Rat Man agrees, but I *am* going to be a father, they say. The sound of this shocks him and he absentmindedly stows the wad of wet in his hip pocket. Now he has announced his part in the whole affair, he wants to be gone. There are other destinies. Being blind and selling matches at street corners. Assisting at an abattoir, but not in rubber gloves. Washing the feet of dictators, Russian, Roman, Papal. Altar boy in lipstick, lighting candles. Dosing himself with viruses to help the future of the race. What he is best at, though, is panic, but who needs a superlative panicker? In Nice, of all places. Panic in Paris, yes, it goes with the overall commotion.

His feet feel glued. His voice has died. His palms pour. A big red iceberg crams his lungs. Headless, he worries with his knees, which twitch in a trap. Now he knows how his parents felt when the Nazis gunned them down, back in the village that ended like a sigh. He does not go. He cannot stay. He is just not very good at frogs, rabbits, and thrushes, but he fishes out the wad of paper and, siting it between his teeth, rhythmically bites on it, as if to forestall a fit. Soon he has bitten it through and has to mold it into one again, half hoping some shape will emerge for which he can take the credit, and those sitting nibbling and sipping around him will exclaim: An owl, at last. A dragon. A man.

Only on a walled-in balcony would he feel safe. He clamps the wad between his teeth again, but he no longer chews. He is going to swallow it soon, he knows, and with it all the contrariness and hurt of the seething world. He tries to shape a baby, but ends up with a breast, which he nervously ruins as soon as made. A roundish ball, the lump now changes hands until an indignant father-to-be swats it back into Poussif's lap.

Poussif nods, he has heard of disease, and is popularly regarded as being one, though the cure is simple. Stay away from him. How he would like to be away from them all, never to come back, even to Sharli, but managing to re-create in Nice, if he has to, the Street of the Cat Who Fishes.

Which is where?

Paris, in a run-down area so ugly it breaks the photographer's lenses and boils the Polaroid developer. That bad. Cozy as an old sock, and with no room for sucklings, tots, toddlers, little feet, floppy legs, baby caca. Nazis he can cope with in his choosily extreme way, but nothing else. Off his trolley, into a good old-fashioned conniption fit. He has the look of a man whose heart is going to stop.

At two in the morning they wake him where he sits, in an upright chair, and rudely announce the safe arrival of a normal male. A Charles, he thinks, and this at once complicates his imagination. A Sharli-boy? A girl he might have been able to take, through a whole series of minor analogies, but a boy is going to split his love of life right down the middle.

They look almost dead as soon as out, he tells her with his fist to his mouth to keep the wrong words back. Death, in prospect gross, in experience faint, in retrospect a nothing.

Look again, Sharli murmurs.

He reports something rubbery in the skin, a hint of surliness in the suck-trimmed mouth.

Home tomorrow, she says, and his world dissolves. One night's sleep and then I'll be as good as new. Poussif is not listening. He has to plan.

If I'm there, he whispers to neither mother nor child.

Whyever not? Her laugh has an edge that misses him. We'll all go soon, anyway. Paris will still be there. End of the school year. She sighs hugely.

End of something, anyway. His gesture includes Warsaw and Atlantis, Pompeii and Lidice. He means it to.

If you have to see it that way.

No answer from Poussif the Rat Man, but his face quivers electrically, his hands pursue each other without catching up. Some almost appeased affliction deep within him has become red-hot. He sees a continent of worry ahead, another boy become cannon fodder. No, he does not know, he does not know how to save anyone at all. All he has ever seen is things not working as they should. As, sometimes, with what he thinks of somberly as his left-hand leg. As with the shipyard worker who fell asleep in the hull of a submarine and was sealed in there forever, in between bulkheads, his corpse sailing the underseas in a limp waltz. It is not something to tell Sharli about, any more than what he thinks about his coming retirement.

Retire, she said. *What from?*

What he says is something he has read, yet not much cared about since. Well, I have lived more than a hundred years in this century, and I expect no more good to come of it.

Not to worry, she says gently. This, my old conscience-on-legs, is a baby, not an Adolf. There's nothing to be afraid of anymore. They'll never come for *us.*

They get you anyway, he says in his best sedate, maternity-ward mumble. Now there's original wisdom for you.

Out he goes, fonder of guillotines than of cradles, of rats than of broken nights, of imaginary beings made of fuzz than of mothers in labor. He nonetheless goes home, on foot, as a Rat Man should to his own funeral. He arrives in a lather of sweat and at once sorts, re-sorts, arranges and rearranges towels, diapers, pads, cloths, soaps, lotions, powders, on table and shelf and bed. Amid this newly created but hygienic muddle, he is an unwholesome graft, a has-been, a leftover, a runt. Naming all his new roles in a vituperative whisper, he decides to pack his things and go. But he has none, except the walking stick, the second fox fur, the doll's house. His most precious possession is a brave front.

Yet he wonders. Is he pretending to zealous fret when what he truly feels is jealousy? Terminally ousted. This is how kings have it. When they abdicate. Or an old elephant. The lion of the pride. No, the most venerable lion. Him. Cock of the walk as was. What he cannot fathom is why death, that old trimming, so sure of getting you, uses a dozen maladies to knock you off with, when any single one would do. Overkill, he says, the whole bloody universe goes in for it. I'd be just as willing to die of jealousy or boredom as of them plus, let's see, what'd a nice little family of ailments be? Arthritis, colic, pneumonia, cancer, lockjaw, hiatus hernia. Death is just the blight over the horizon, no more intentional than a shower of thorns, but, Lord, how it skulks, how insecure it is.

When baby cries, Rat Man cries, more huskily. When baby burps, so does he. And when baby writhes, he too pretends to be wet or messed. Change me, Sharli, he wails with his broadest, foulest grin. They sleep apart, as before the birth, she tucked in bed with baby. Poussif wants to suck, he says. Burp me, Sharli. Powder my bum. It's formula time. Mix me a warm one now. You can bring us up together, like twins. Big twin, little twin, until one of us pops off. I'll wheel him around all year.

Not in that pissoir on wheels you won't. But all he answers with is what seems a poem, a song, a snatch of music-hall ditty. Is this what his mother murmured when his father leaked baby Poussif into her while she yearned for him to get it over with?

Dans une cage
Sur la plage
Du Moyen Age
Il y avait une orage
*Sage . . .**

She says nothing, bewildered by what might from someone less extremist be a birth poem. He looks at her: merry-plump, ripe with matronly sophistication. She seems somehow graver. That is right, he thinks; she should. He gets up in the night. Changes little Charles, whom he has suggested calling De Gaulle. He even waits around at bath time, a golem at the font, a monster of basin rectitude. Fumble, curse, and dither as he may, he more or less gets it right during yet another personable doldrum that has come his way unbidden. The via Via he calls it. Maybe he should go out after Barbie full blast

* In a cage/on the beach/of the Middle Ages/there was a wise storm . . .

now, simply on behalf of everyone else. He'll take and dispatch a Nazi hostage at random. Yes. Never let a good thing go to waste. Waste not, he believes, and die never. It needn't even be Barbie, although he's the nearest. Any one of the damned will do.

Picture him, unshaven, folding up the soiled diapers, testing the bath water with his very tongue, or enfolding Rat Man Two in an apricot shawl for sleep. Lugubriously tender, no more a lover than he is a regular on TV, he begins to see the way to go while Sharli notices only a new tautness in his demeanor, a touch of mellow huff. He tidies up, as ever, and even learns to answer the phone without clearing his throat nonstop, without trembling out of his skin. He is building up to his second call, although the first, for the taxi, almost finished him off.

Next thing, she thinks, he will get a checkbook and a little calculator: prelude to solvency. But she knows him too little, thinks him a half-human thirsting for completeness whereas he thirsts to go the other way, back to Cain and Abel. He is warming up on little Charles, not vicious, dissembling, or rough, but very much within himself, awaiting the last phase of his awful glory. He yearns for impact on the way things are.

Alas, he even becomes confident enough to take the baby to his fountain at night, and when she at last runs him down, going there in the Citroën but not running him over with it, there he is by his broom, with her baby wrapped in dark green plastic, fast asleep in the finger-deep slop. She yells, but she has no words, not much breath, so she points, makes a fist, holds the heels of her hands a hairsbreadth from his eyes, then takes the baby away, her head thundering from lack of sleep and a new sense of how haphazard a betrayal can be.

He builds a cradle from orange boxes, but she will not let the baby near, so he waits until she is asleep, then tucks him in and rocks the cradle with his viscous coo. He almost likes the rumpled, milky face; he can see it at the end of a fox fur on a stick, or nestled within his coat to startle passersby.

Borrow the vacuum cleaner, she says, from the neighbor, and do the floor. She has to teach, and Poussif has to babysit. Yet such is not his way, although he agrees. Knock at the door of a stranger, introduce himself as either Poussif the father or Rat Man the old celebrity, and then ask for what is rightly his or hers or theirs? He will no more do this than journey to the Massif Central and tap against its flank, asking in. Indeed, he would more readily do that, wanting a subterranean race of Rat Men to greet him in the bowels of the chalk.

So as not to wake the baby, but also to save himself from the scene at the neighbor's door, he rummages around and finds a roll of sticky tape larger than his outsize hand. Next he hunts a thing of length, and soon selects the walking stick. To this he adds a two-meter length of tape, sticky side out, a vague manila-hued rose of loops and furls, and now begins to lift up lint, pressing the face of the rose vertically down, then, as hair and fluff accumulate, rolling it along the rug. After he has done this a dozen times, not peeling away the used tape but adding a new length each time, he has a shabby candy floss.

This he sets aside and begins to layer the floor with parallel, partly overlapping strips, a dozen at a time, which he hauls up with a ringmaster's motion, wondering if this is plastic surgery. Ask the floor to wait and then hand it a mirror, saying: Just as good as new. This is the Stone Age way of cleaning up. It is quieter for baby too. He likes the stealth of it, the solemn bend and crouch he has to do, like planting a field in reverse. Up they come, the crumbs and the bits of broken toothpick, the whorls of hair, the threads fallen from a hem or the lip of a new shirt's pocket, even the shreds of paper and the silver foil shed from rolls of pungent British mints that have no center hole and bear the aloof, lordly name Trebor, which he thinks the name of some ancient

Saxon hero: Trebor like Horatius on his epic bridge, or the Dutch boy with his finger in the dike.

Fatigue halts him. All this up and down has made his blood flow wrong. Giving it a chance to smooth out and pick up normal speed, he lies full length on the linty floor beneath the bed. One day, he knows it, having mentally rehearsed the whole event, he will let them take his blood pressure and flood his veins with the same substance as makes rats bleed to death. Once upon a time it, or something like it, grew in the wild, a clover that even turns cows into bleeders. All this to thin his blood. He sighs, already weary with the thought of medication he will never take unless force-fed it in Intensive Care, which to him is not so much a place to go as an occupation, a habit, he has had lifelong, practicing it, like a cow or a rat, in the wild, with no help from anyone. Making it up as he went along. Getting it wrong, doubtless. True, he tells himself, knowing he soon must sleep, once they get their hands on you, they stuff you full of pills you dare not ever stop taking, or you drop dead while buying a newspaper. Once they have you, they have you by the short hairs. Better to be a creaking gate for a hundred years, Rat Man, than do yourself in with ratsbane.

When his blood pools in the bottom of his heart, making a bulge, he thinks he has a pear in his chest. At least that's how the heart feels that comes to his mind's eye. When he's horizontal, he thinks his heart has the shape of an ice bag, round but flat with the blood gently swilling around on pointless journeys. From an almost complete halt he thus advances to going in circles. His pulse is a fidget rather than the sign of any serious, life-supporting activity, and this is true of him either standing or lying down. He feels like a sponge, having the tides tug him this way and that. He seems to be wobbling about within his outline. Oh mercy, he hears himself droning, I did my stuff today. Please let it not be even monthly after this. Dozing, he feels made of suet, lacking bone and muscle. Now the cotless baby cries. *Le Grand Charles.* Charles the Great. Charlemagne. De Gaulle is best. De Gaulle of Gaul. Again something epic assails and wins him. This is the baby of babies. He brews the formula and cools it with his breath. Then he nestles him and plugs the well-scrubbed nipple in. He is both sexes today, Poussif. All ages. It is as if he has put the nipple to himself, with his momma on the other end of it, doodling at the piano while giving suck. Madame R. was breastless.

He longs for when he retires, and they live on a soup of mustard in hot water, bread filched from bird boxes, sardines wrestled from neighborhood cats, giveaway hors d'oeuvres from the supermarkets, peanuts from the grandest of the airlines, dandelion salad, grass porridge, and the ultimate sandwich, which is a slice of bread pointed one way between two slices both pointed the other. Known among the poor as right-angle wad.

His coarse and willful vision of things to come seduces him, but he also succumbs to something else. Coursing through him, unbidden and unwanted, come tremors of cool devotedness. The jealousy, if that, has gone, and all he feels is wise, paternal competence, with afternoon television murmuring at him, his blood no longer a stammer just beneath his skin.

Rat Man dozes. Poussif wakes. Baby sleeps again. Odd, he muses, how that other side of him, the bloodthirsty boulevardier, died into Poussif the ordinary chap. The two of him are one. A toff has turned into a daddy. He is all emotion, like a Crusader with red cross on white shield, and satin robes billowing behind as he rides down Huns.

All through the afternoon they doze ensemble, he on the floor, De Gaulle under the pale blue comforter bought with money earned on the boulevards of Paris. *His* idea, this. The truth is otherwise. Even the color is right. How did Sharli know? He sees a future of nothing but this.

Why, this is worth killing for.

When at last he rises, he collects up the twists of sticky

tape, tugs the rose off the walking stick, and advances upon the doorway of the bedroom, sliding the stick around the corner, as ever, not to scare but to amaze. The baby sees nothing, but Poussif sees himself in the tall mirror, advancing and hovering into a halt as, not with a fox's head this time, he seems to port a lance. The sentry. The guardian. The home help with a sword. The boy who decades ago hid under the floorboards while his parents died in the village church, and then fled with his cap and satchel, has turned into Trebor the lint collector and— He pauses. What else? A postilion, whom lightning dare not strike. The thought soothes him. He removes all sticky tape from sight and dumps it in the trash, yet not before juggling the tacky light ball from hand to hand. He tries to toss it up, it will not go. He pulls it from one hand to the other. It sticks. He wrenches it loose with a motion so slight as hardly to make contact at all, and it comes away. Up it goes. It lands on his upturned face and lodges there like manna. Frail and honey-sticky.

Who in the world would wish to imitate him and his feeble link with the race? I am on my own, he decides. I have come a long way. Where did all my gusto go?

It has soared into the sky without so much as his name on it and is wafting along all the radials pointing away from him. Rat Man was never here, among babies and jet engines whining like creatures unfed. They're both unfed. He will never take De Gaulle to the touchdown, lift-off, point, to hear the grand gulp of the jets. We'll never poison *you,* he says, your lungs are soft and tiny, pink and new. In days to come, though, we'll make a tiny runway on the rug, right here, with model planes and a small cozy terminal, with tapes of the real thing called Airport Sounds. We'll have parallel runways, Left and Right, and tiny wind socks made of tissue paper blown out straight by the wind from the electric fan. We'll move the fan around to change the wind's direction, and we'll either lie at ground level or look down on things from up on the couch. And you, you can lie on the runway itself, aligned with the traffic and more permanent than wind. His mind roves about, embellishing the plan, which now includes a doll's house, a fox in hiding in woodlands made of sponge green-painted, and tiny wooden deer nibbling in the shade or, at dusk in summer, airing their flanks as the sun droops.

Aware of his need to stage things, always to mount some kind of show against the tidal wave of history, he keeps it vague. Just so long as there is room to move in, a space to sign his name, to ply his rat, to wheel his pram, to set up his guillotine either full-scale or reduced, he will be happy to muddle along.

Rallentando. One of his mother's words, it meant, it means, relenting, loosening your grip, whereas *deponent,* surely a word of his father's, meant quitting to die. All I am, he now knows, is a smudge, a smear, a blur, hardly a source of light for someone over yonder peering for signs of brainy life. Yet what you were goes on glowing and can be seen by other breeds of folk. The goblins out there. The globe-headed elves. The lizards with books for brains. The geniuses with no feet and radio eyes. How wonderful to meet them, though lopsidedly, eternities later, as they pick up the little man-stain, the slightly smaller but more colorful woman-stain, the tiny squiggle of the baby. They monitor our home-made dream, watching us dab the floor, our faces, load the nipple into baby's mouth, and put the house to sleep at night with a little tear-shaped switch. Off or on. Faint, esteemed, muddled beings: that's how the goblins in Andromeda will see us. Not worth a helping hand, but then none of them anymore exist. This is their glowworm saying *yours.*

His second phone call will be from sickness to health, collect. He will become a trashcomber wherever they settle, filching aluminum cans from among others' leavings with a long hooked stick, then crushing them on end with his heel. Done. When he has a hundred, turn them in for cash, thus connected with the mouths of at least a hundred souls. The prospects are gigantic. In time, he will reach more in this way than even Rat Man ever reached. And, in his cups, he will tell stories about drugged greyhounds, their speed, their lazy runs, their seizures in the kennels. Nearer to home, he will open books wide to let the ideas out, and set them down, leaving them to flap their wings like birds, and, as he moves about the living room, he will revel in how the bulk of his body chokes and blurs the signal, making a buzz, a drone, picking himself up on radar by accident.

Twenty-one

Should the earth quake again, he knows exactly what to do. Strip up the floorboards one by one until the gap will take a crib without chafing the sides. Then, with baby De Gaulle tucked deep into his bower, Poussif alias no one anymore will march out into the street, give himself up to the Huns, and let them have their way with him at last. That long-delayed burning. He will no longer care about the smooth tanned wrist amending the record on the neatly stacked pages of cream-laid paper, turning fact into fantasy, victim into hero, fixing on the garish things in his life. It will be as if that gentle, devious ghost had never been, and his defensive murmurings had all of them gone unheard, all his heartsick improvisations. No more iron in his mask. All his dithers, his fumbles, his loving, wished away by a bold, heroic thumb-print from his last adieu, which he makes with his fist held aloft, the thumb upright.